Candlelight
Ecstasy Romance®

HER ENTIRE BEING FOCUSED ON THE MASTERLY HANDS THAT STROKED AND CARESSED. . . .

She was starved for love, but now, as Charles traced erotic paths, discovering the inches of skin that brought the most response, she realized she was in danger of letting a decade of desire destroy her carefully laid plans.

Mentally she recited the litany that had become the driving force in her life: "I want a child. I want a child, not a husband, not a lover, only . . . a child."

"What's wrong?" Charles asked hoarsely. His lips drew her breath into his body as though by doing so he could replenish it with his own fiery heat. "It's too late to stop, Johanna. God, what do you want if not this?" he whispered against her throat.

"I want you . . ." Johanna mumbled into the crispness of his hair. "I want you to give me a child."

A CANDLELIGHT ECSTASY ROMANCE®

TAKING A CHANCE

Anna Hudson

A CANDLELIGHT ECSTASY ROMANCE®

Published by
Dell Publishing Co., Inc.
1 Dag Hammarskjold Plaza
New York, New York 10017

Dell ® TM 681510, Dell Publishing Co., Inc.

Candlelight Ecstasy Romance®, 1,203,540, is a registered
trademark of Dell Publishing Co., Inc., New York,
New York.

ISBN: 0-440-18482-7

Printed in the United States of America

First printing—May 1984

Taking a Chance is dedicated to those who missed.

Missed

Young memories are born of love.
Too soon you whisper to your departing love,
"Miss you."

Practical memories are built with another.
Still you whisper to your absent love,
"Missing you."

Old memories are frayed by time.
Too late you whisper to your unrequited love,
"Missed you."

To Our Readers:

We have been delighted with your enthusiastic response to Candlelight Ecstasy Romances®, and we thank you for the interest you have shown in this exciting series.

In the upcoming months we will continue to present the distinctive sensuous love stories you have come to expect only from Ecstasy. We look forward to bringing you many more books from your favorite authors and also the very finest work from new authors of contemporary romantic fiction.

As always, we are striving to present the unique, absorbing love stories that you enjoy most—books that are more than ordinary romance.

Your suggestions and comments are always welcome. Please write to us at the address below.

Sincerely,

The Editors
Candlelight Romances
1 Dag Hammarskjold Plaza
New York, New York 10017

CHAPTER ONE

The small beam of light penetrated deep into her cornea. Johanna Jenkins, trying to appear composed, relaxed her life and death grip on the black armrest. Her palms perspired, betraying the nervousness she felt at having her first love within kissing distance.

"Look to the left, please." Charles Franklin, optometrist, demanded softly.

Quickly, Johanna obeyed.

"Still playing games?" the doctor asked quietly in the soft-spoken voice of a lover.

"I beg your pardon?"

Leaning back, he pushed a button, and the dark interior of the examination room burst into light. "You are Johanna Jenkins, aren't you?" His dark blue eyes glinted mischievously. His smile exposed the dimple Johanna had caressed years ago and had fantasized about repeatedly since her divorce.

Her pupils contracted involuntarily, just as her heart skipped a beat in anticipation.

"I thought you didn't recognize me," she responded, smoothing the skirt of her classic navy blue summer suit.

His chuckle, which she well remembered, increased the amount of moisture on her palms.

"And if I hadn't, my 'first love' would have sedately exited from my life. Right?" Charles shook his head, causing a dark lock of straight brown hair to fall haphazardly across his forehead.

Johanna smiled nervously.

"Probably," she answered truthfully.

Charles Franklin stood, and his athletic grace of twenty years ago was still evident as he strode casually to the dark walnut desk. "Examination over. Relax and come over here." He gestured toward the comfortable lounge chair placed beside the desk.

With practiced poise, Johanna moved to the chair, gracefully lowering herself into the earth-tone cushions. Her confidence, which had been severely damaged by her divorce, was partially restored by the admiration evident in Charles's glance as he examined her from her casual, short hairstyle to her well-shod toes.

"You look fantastic. Much better than I'd expect."

"What did you expect? A dowdy matron?" she asked, slightly miffed.

"I don't know what I expected, but when I look in the mirror I find that getting older doesn't always mean getting better," he answered wryly, smoothing back the errant lock of hair that had hidden a slightly receding hairline.

"You look fantastic," she quickly injected, waving aside his self-deprecating statement with a flick of the wrist.

Charles chuckled and said, "Now that we've admired each other, how about getting reacquainted? I've a million and one questions to ask that have absolutely nothing to do with those lovely eyes."

Elated, Johanna answered, "Just name the time and place. I'm curious about you, too!" *Don't sound so eager,* she silently chastised herself. *You're thirty-four, not sixteen.*

"Some place intimate for dinner?" he asked, his eyes sweeping to the deep vee of her white blouse.

"My house?" Johanna suggested. What could be more intimate and inviting than a cozy dinner for two in her own home? Her scheme was on course. *Full steam ahead,* she thought.

"Will your husband mind?" She knew what he was really asking—was there a husband on the home front?

"I'm divorced . . . no children, no ties. The classic career woman." One red-tipped fingernail traced over her lips, trying to stop the next statement before it slipped out. "Bring Susan, by all means."

The dreaded name that had come between them during their college years flowed over her tongue fluidly. Charles couldn't know what it had cost to casually drop the name of the woman he'd preferred and married. When she'd started this project, the gossip she had gathered had not informed her of his present marital status, but she hoped—no, prayed—he was free.

"Susan is dead. Killed in a car accident." A flash of pain puckered his brow. "Over ten years ago," he added.

"I'm sorry," she said softly. "I hadn't heard."

"We were living in Texas at the time it happened." He paused. Johanna could see him trying to pull away from the hurt and pain of the memories.

"A lot of things happened in Texas I'd like to forget," he mumbled.

"So we're both alone," she deduced. *And lonely,* she could have added.

The boyish grin he flashed brought the mood back to the joy of rediscovery. "Not always alone. I've lived with two women since Suzy died."

Johanna tried to cover the shock of his disclosure with a flippant question. "Are you betwixt and between women now?"

"Yes, between. Care to fill the vacancy?"

Teasing mockery let her know that she had not succeeded in masking the shock to her strict middle-class upbringing. The concept of living with a man stretched her moral fiber past the breaking point. Subconsciously she had wanted to revive her love for Charles because he was part of the unwritten code she'd been raised with. Had Charles walked away from their common values? Had he changed the way Bill had?

Why had the derogatory word "cheating" been changed to the romantic "love affair"? Johanna had certainly felt cheated when Bill's indiscreet "love affair" had been uncovered. She had ignored the first marital slip, finding excuses for his infidelity. Only when he had flaunted and taunted, using explicit descriptions of his multiple extramarital relations, had Johanna made the emotional break and hired an attorney to start divorce proceedings.

"No, thanks." Johanna responded primly. "But the invitation for dinner still holds." If Charles *had* changed life-styles, what was the cause? Curiosity whetted her appetite. For what she had in mind, perhaps it would be better for his morals to have lapsed.

"Fine. I'll get your address off the patient card. Speaking as your eye doctor, have you considered soft contact lenses? You'd be a perfect candidate," he enthused.

"I've never considered contacts. Don't they hurt?"

"Only at first," he answered, then teased, "sort of like sex. After the first time you try it you wouldn't go back to anything else."

Heat flushed through Johanna. How many times had they spoken of her virginal state during that fateful summer before he had married Susan? Kissing and light petting hadn't been enough for Charles, but he had been too . . . honorable to go beyond the limits she'd set. Of course, she had broader views now, at thirty-four, having been married. He was right. She disliked going backward. But her marriage had taught her that overactive hormones didn't lead to happy marriages.

" 'Try it, you'll like it' applies to sex *and* contacts?"

They both laughed heartily at the comparison.

"Well, think about it, anyway," Charles said, rising to his feet.

"Which? Sex or contacts?" Johanna asked, delighted at the opportunity to tease him with his own words. As she rose from the chair, she felt the soft hairs on her arm stand on end as Charles draped his arm across her shoulders.

"Both," he murmured close to her ear. "You've already put a definite stress on my professional ethics code."

Charles hesitated, then, turning Johanna toward him, he said, "I'm glad you came back into my life, Johanna. I've thought about you often."

"In your dreams, Chuck?" she asked, using his high school nickname.

Charles tossed his head back and laughed uproariously. "No one has called me Chuck in years. I love it."

"I think of you as Chuck . . . my first love," she answered seriously, revealing more than she'd intended. Bowing her head, she avoided seeing his reaction.

His hands cupped her face, lifting it, as his thumbs stroked her lower lip with a painfully sensuous touch. She couldn't raise her eyes above the lips she longed to caress.

"Johanna, sweet, Johanna . . ." she heard as

his lips grazed her cheek. His arms held her gently, tenderly, as though she were an illusion. Her arms circled his waist, and the feeling of finally having come home after an arduous journey washed over her. Johanna pressed against him, basking in the glow of love's fire kindled, banked, then relit. Its brightness was heightened by the years of separation.

A persistent rapping at the door behind them made Charles ease reluctantly away.

"Doctor?" they heard through the door, "your three-fifteen is here."

"Okay, Betty. Put Mr. Jorgeson in room B. Talk to him about his German Shepherd," he instructed, speaking now with professional briskness.

His blue eyes never left her face. Sighing heavily, he shook his head. When the straying dark lock fell forward again, the temptation was too strong to resist, and Johanna brushed it back into place. His smile, dimple, and the crinkly laugh lines around his eyes rewarded the intimate touch.

"Seven o'clock all right?" he asked, opening the door and politely ushering Johanna out.

"Fine," she answered, hoping the hours would pass swiftly. "See you then."

The heat and humidity, typical of a St. Louis summer, was overwhelming when she left

Charles's office. Had it been snowing in July, she wouldn't have noticed. Her smile of satisfaction couldn't be affected by weather.

Driving from the Chesterfield Mall back toward the city, the stereo tape recorder softly played love ballads, which kept the gentle curve on her lips. The strains of Barry Manilow's "Somewhere Down the Road" reassured Johanna that she'd been right to get in touch with Charles. She, not someone else, was directing the course of her life.

Momentarily the smile drooped when she recounted their meeting. Her romantic fantasies had included a passionate embrace immediately upon her entry into the office. Johanna chuckled. The Chuck she'd known might have reacted that way, but the Charles he'd become was too cosmopolitan to fling her on the couch and begin making mad, passionate love.

Johanna wouldn't contemplate the teasing offer he'd made about living together. She laughed aloud at his comparison of contact lenses and sex. Their conversations had always held sexual undertones. That hadn't changed in twenty years. The strong, physical pull toward one another hadn't changed, either.

Bill, her ex-husband, would have croaked if he had seen and heard his "inhibited, prudish, frigid wife." Those were only a few of his favor-

19

ite names for her. Her lack of ardor was Bill's favorite excuse for seeking the companionship of women half his age.

That was *his* problem. Johanna couldn't help wondering if his new wife was busily keeping house, cooking meals, and washing clothes, while Bill pursued the challenge of unconquered women.

Her smile became stilted. That was *their* problem. She couldn't care less. Hurt and pain were in the past. The wounds hopefully were healing, but the scars, though hidden away, were there.

Signaling a right-hand turn, Johanna turned off Olive Street toward her two story, ultramodern condominium. After the divorce, she'd sold the house she'd lived in for ten years. She'd always hated the huge house in Ladue. It had been furnished by a prominent interior decorator. The dark antique furniture, heavy brocade drapes, and expensive ornaments had made the house a showplace befitting the image of a successful attorney Bill wished to project, but the ostentatiousness had never suited her taste. She'd used her share of the equity they had divided after the divorce to pay for the condo. Fortunately she didn't need alimony from Bill. Teaching would never make her rich, but it did provide a modest income, and when supplemented by the monies from her grandfather's estate, it allowed her to live quite comfortably.

The soft chimes heralding Charles's arrival sent Johanna rushing to the front entry hall. The long, golden silk caftan swirled around her slender legs as she made one final inspection before opening the door. The entire condo was decorated in subtle shadings from the cool purity of white to the warm richness of black. The only splashes of color were in the original modernistic oil paintings and sculpture done in a variety of media. Long ceiling-to-floor windows provided light for the multitude of hanging baskets of plants. Air-conditioning vents made fronds of ferns and the trailing leaves of philodendrons sway. Everything was perfect; a study in contrast and harmony.

"Hello, Johanna. May I come in?"

Though she was blocking the entry way, Johanna's flesh quivered and refused to budge. The sudden weakness in her knees threatened her cool facade. How many times had she mentally envisioned this moment? More than a thousand, she was certain. Towering several inches over her, Charles's frame filled the doorway, and his presence filled her heart. She wanted to fling herself into his arms but didn't. Stepping aside she welcomed him into her home.

"Thanks. For a moment I thought we were going to eat on your doorstep," Charles teased as he entered.

Laughing nervously, Johanna invited him into the living room.

"Can I get you something to drink?" she asked, remembering her manners.

"I brought Asti Spumanti. Do you still like it?" he asked, extending a wine bottle wrapped in a white linen napkin.

Charles could have had an elephant in his arms; Johanna wouldn't have noticed. Her eyes were mesmerized by the changing blue of his eyes. Sky blue when she'd opened the door, they'd darkened to midnight blue after glancing over her shimmering gown. His dimple was deep and inviting.

"You feel it, too, don't you?" Charles queried, putting the bottle on the glass-topped coffee table, then removing his suit coat and tossing it on a nearby contemporary wing chair. "I have the same intense desire now that I had twenty years ago when I first met you at Caroline's party. Dance with me, *again*. Let me hold you."

Not hesitating, Johanna stepped into his open arms. The soft music from the radio was reminiscent of the songs they'd heard as teenagers. The same feeling of having come home enveloped her. The tension and fear she'd felt before his arrival evaporated as his arms enveloped her.

"We didn't dance this closely at Caroline's," she said, pulling back slightly, fearing she was being too bold, too eager, too . . . wanton.

"I only knew the box step. I'm not that square now. I prefer gentle swaying." Taking her left hand, he nudged it over his shoulder. "Put your arms around my neck," he instructed softly.

"Mmm, this is definitely better," she replied, loosening her previous inhibitions. This was Charles, her first love. Her dreams were becoming reality. Why fight the closeness and deny the dream?

A piece of plastic wrap couldn't have wedged itself between them. They fit together. Their hearts touched and beat more quickly.

"Johanna?"

"Hmm?" she answered, totally relaxed.

"I'm going to kiss you," he whispered, his warm, clean breath touching her cheek.

The swaying stopped. Charles drew his chest back, but his hands continued to slide rhythmically on her lower hips. Slowly, with careful deliberation, his mouth descended.

Johanna had time to say no. She didn't. She wanted his kiss. Tentatively, his lips touched hers, once, twice, almost as though they were asking, "Is this a dream?"

She'd been kissed the same way years ago. This hadn't changed. Johanna remembered the gentle nibbling. He'd changed his aftershave, though. A musk oil had replaced Old Spice. The nibbling halted. He seemed confident of her response; the kiss deepened, lips sealed together.

Rubbing the tips of her fingers against collar, skin, and bristly hairs at the nape of his neck, she enjoyed the erotic change of textures. How often she'd stroked this same strong column. One hand cupped the side of his closely shaven face. It was different from the smooth skin she'd once run fingertips over. It felt good . . . masculine.

One finger caressed the indentation on his cheek. She'd teased him years ago saying God had placed a finger there and said, "I love you." It had become her gesture that meant I love you, too. His tongue slipped between her lips, acknowledging her touch. Their mouths mingled in a sweetness that hadn't changed. Charles explored, renewing his knowledge of all the secret crevices with a swirling, flickering probe.

A deep groan came from Charles. Molding her closer with the strength of one arm, his other hand barely touched the silk covering her round, firm breast. His thumb circled the tip, which pressed against the lacy, restraining bra.

Johanna was lost in memories. They could

have been standing at her parents' front door or lying side by side in the backseat of his old Ford. She wanted him as much now as she had then, but at thirty-four, having been married, she wanted to ease the flames burning deep within her.

Charles's manliness hardened against her slightly rounded stomach. Steel against silk. Once they had both been ashamed of their unconcealable arousal. He couldn't keep it from happening and she couldn't avoid noticing. Then, not now, he would abruptly draw away as though to continue would be abhorrent to her. They were different now . . . as was the music.

Elvis, at his loudest, blared from the radio. "Don't You Step on My Blue Suede Shoes" came close to making the speakers thump off the glass shelf.

Recovering first, Charles began the intricate steps of a fast dance routine. Johanna giggled as she was twirled one way, then the other. They improvised as they used to at dances held in their high school gymnasium.

Panting from the strenuous, fast pace, they collapsed on the white leather sofa, joined together by laughter rather than passion. Johanna enjoyed the dance but regretted Elvis's upbeat intrusion on their lovemaking.

"That's for all the Elvis fans," the disc jockey

shouted, "King of Rock and Roll. Tuned up, turned on, and shouting it out for the music lovers of the fifties."

"From all the songs Elvis recorded, why did he choose that one?" Johanna groaned. Getting off the sofa, she crossed to the stereo, turned off the radio, and clicked in a tape of love songs.

"That was quite a trip down memory lane. Only the order was reversed. We danced, made out, then I went home and took a cold shower." Eyes twinkling merrily, he grimaced, then asked, "Did you hear the old alarm bell ringing when I was getting ready to make the big move?"

"The big move?" she asked, faking innocence.

"Unsnapping . . . your . . . bra," he answered, eyes shining, chuckles separating the words.

"I seem to recall the alarm system being defunct on a few occasions," Johanna quipped cheekily.

"Damned few! Four to be exact!"

"You counted?" she asked, astonished not only because he had kept score, but also because he had remembered.

"Honey, all the other guys were busy counting 'going all the way.'" He laughed in self-deprecation as his eyebrow lifted upward. "Did you manage to save yourself for the marital bed?" he asked, reaching for wine.

Not wanting him to see the flush that spread over her face, Johanna pivoted toward the glass cabinet and extracted long-stemmed crystal from the top shelf as she decided to be truthful.

"As a matter of fact, I did. My wedding night was a disaster, and believe you me, I heard about it right up until the final decree." Although she tried to answer his question lightly, the old bitterness crept in.

When she turned, Charles was one step behind her, his eyes searching her face. The midnight blue blaze questioned the pain in her voice.

"It would be good between us, honey. I want you more than I've wanted any woman for years," his deep voice coaxed, while his eyes promised what they had denied each other so long ago.

Would it be? she thought silently. Bill had never even tried to make sex enjoyable for her. Sex had been humiliated, degraded, the worst part of marriage. Charles had aroused her more in ten minutes of dancing than Bill had during their entire marriage.

No! her pride shouted louder than any warning bell, *don't take a chance. Use him just as you have been used, you fool.* Johanna turned her head away, shaking it solemnly.

"No, Chuck."

Instead of being angry at the curt rebuff, Charles tossed back his head and roared with laughter. He put his arms around her as he put his head on her shoulder and continued to laugh.

Johanna stomped his toe hard enough to be felt but not hard enough to hurt. "Quit laughing at me!"

"Can't help it," he gasped. Breathing deeply, he straightened and expelled the last gust of laughter into the air. "I must have heard that exact same line, in that exact same voice, a million times. Honey, I'm light-years away from 'Chuck.'" The humor left his face. "Don't call me that again unless you're wrapped in my arms and your body is sheathing mine. Then you can shout my name in ecstasy." He lowered his head to Johanna's ear, nuzzled the dark, wavy hair aside, and nipped her delicate earlobe, which emphasized his meaning.

Removing the stemware from her hands, he left her standing there, not knowing her heart was thumping erratically as she touched the ear he had bitten. She ran shaking hands over her breasts trying to calm her breathing. "My God," she whispered, "he may be able to help me more than I planned."

CHAPTER TWO

Admitting even to herself that she was sexually frustrated was more than she felt comfortable with. This was pure, unadulterated lust. Chuck had been her childhood sweetheart, but could she still love him? *My body sure does,* she answered mentally. *No, that's just lust!* Johanna smiled. "I wonder if cold showers work," she muttered.

"Didn't your mother ever tell you that only crazy people talk to themselves?" Charles teased. "That's one reason I prefer having someone live with me. It's someone to . . . talk to." His broad leer, and the way he twisted an imaginary handlebar mustache, made a giggle slip through her lips.

"And what about the intimate dinner you promised?" he asked, grabbing her hand and leading her toward the aroma wafting from the oven.

"*Dinner* was all I promised," she retorted playfully, tugging on his arm to slow down his pace.

"Can I help? I'm quite domesticated . . . at times," he said with a broad wink.

Did men help in the kitchen? She was used to waiting hand and foot on Bill while he tapped the table with his knife and fork.

"Pour the wine and light the candles while I get the dinner out of the oven," she instructed succinctly.

With a companionable nod of assent, he headed toward the dining room. When Johanna entered, the room was dark except for the candles' glow. Flickering, they shone on the sterling silver and glimmered off the crystal. Charles stood by one chair waiting to seat her.

"You're one lovely hostess, honey," he murmured as he pulled out the chair, and waited while she placed the casserole dish in its silver holder. The compliment was unexpected.

"Thank you. You're a charming guest," she said, returning the compliment as best she could. She wasn't used to receiving them, and she felt the blood rush to her face as she watched Charles seat himself.

After serving the salad, they began filling the void the years had left.

"Tell me about Johanna Jenkins," Charles inquired.

"There's not much to tell. I graduated from college with a B.A. degree in History and English. Since then I've been teaching."

She wished she could relate adventuresome tales about an exciting, glamorous career, or perhaps a dramatic success story about climbing the corporate ladder. The truth was simple; she was a born teacher. She loved it.

"And I examine eyes." Charles carefully placed his fork on the salad plate. His eyes glowed, taking on a silver cast in the candlelight. "What district do you teach in?"

As she named the district, she watched his eyebrows rise.

"That's the district that's been illegally on strike, isn't it?" he asked with a grin.

"Three times," she affirmed, serving the seafood casserole.

"Ever walk the picket line?" he asked.

"Um-hummm," she answered. "Striking is a rare experience. There are three hundred fifty-seven paces between the two central office driveways." Johanna chuckled.

"Why the laughter?"

"You're looking at a rabble-rousing ringleader, a disgrace to the profession," she answered, the battle fire burning in her dark eyes. "Those were the *kind* words. I was threatened with being fired, spending my remaining years teaching in the cafeteria, and my life was anonymously threatened." *Maybe my life isn't as dull as I'd thought,* she mused. She didn't think of herself as a heroine, and she certainly had no desire to be a martyr. Before the strike she'd been described as a dedicated professional, which in layman's language meant she was being poorly paid for a strenuous job.

When she glanced up from her plate, she was surprised at the consternation that made deep creases on Charles's forehead.

"Well, at least your husband was here to protect you."

Johanna strangled as her throat closed on a piece of shrimp. Coughing spasmodically, she cleared the blockage, but her eyes glistened with moisture from the irony of Charles's assumption.

"Bill's law firm represented the school board," she replied, a mirthless laugh accompanying the disclosure.

"That's rough," he commiserated thoughtfully.

Not wanting to discuss the ugliness the strike had brought into her marriage, she asked, "Am I wrong in thinking there's more to your story?"

A broad smile lifted the corners of his generous mouth. His dimple became a dark shadow in the shallow candlelight. "Very perceptive. I lucked into getting a few patents on some optometrist tools. Between my practice, which specializes in hard-to-fit lenses, and patent royalties, I keep the bill collectors away from the door."

The modest reply made him rise further in her esteem. In the past year she had heard grandiose boasting from the small selection of men she had dated. It was refreshing to have to drag information out of a man rather than have it splashed over her like cheap perfume.

"We're among the fortunate," Charles summarized. "We both love our jobs. Believe me, it's a rarity."

Johanna turned her face toward the dark window to avoid letting him see the expression she knew was spreading over her face. Her official letter of resignation, received and accepted by the school board, stood between Johanna and her career. She had let them believe she was a victim of teacher "burn-out," but she knew better. Loving, instructing, watching other people's children grow had become a burden rather than a joy. Her goals had changed.

"Coffee?" she offered, realizing that while she had been woolgathering, he had finished the main course.

"I'll get it. You finish up," he answered, gathering the dishes he had used and taking them into the kitchen.

The man is a marvel, she thought, watching his long strides into the kitchen. The sound of water running and the dishwasher door dropping forward was unbelievable to her ears. Had he rinsed them and loaded them into the dishwasher? *Wonders will never cease!*

"If you're through, why don't you serve the coffee in the living room and I'll finish clearing off the table," he suggested, placing the coffee urn on a hot pad.

"Leave them. I'll do them later," she replied, then added, "Guests aren't supposed to do kitchen duty."

"Am I only a guest?" he asked, baiting the trap.

"Of course not, but—" she began.

The snare closed. "Then be a good girl and let me help. After all, you did prepare dinner, so it's the least I can do." Pulling out her chair, his lips brushed against her hair. "If the old cliché about the stomach being the path to a man's heart is true, you're headed in the right direction."

The lavish compliment was, she felt, more than the food deserved, but when she looked at his face she could see he was truly sincere. Flustered, she picked up the urn, cups and saucers, placed them on a silver tray, and moved into the living area.

"Besides," she heard from the kitchen, "if we're going to live together, I have to do my share."

Live together bounced and echoed, mingling with the romantic strains of music, blending as though belonging.

"Not in this lifetime, mister!" she muttered, unwilling to accept such a drastic change in her strategy. She needed him to reach her ultimate goal but only for a short time.

Johanna poured the coffee, topping it off with Asbach Uralt. The blend of bitter, dark coffee with the sweet warmth of the German brandy was better than any dessert. Sinking into the down-filled leather cushions on the sofa, she closed her eyes as she idly stirred the coffee with a silver spoon. It was pure luxury to have the dishes done by someone else. Lips and toes curled upward, a feeling of languishing contentment spread through her bones as she heard the first cycle of the dishwasher begin.

On reflection, Johanna realized that if Charles wanted to live with her, at least he wouldn't object to helping her reach her goal—having a child. Obviously neither of them wanted the emotional drain or the demands of loving, sharing, being dependent on each other. When the time was right, she'd ask him, but later. Let the physical pull, the attraction, whatever, take over for now. As though summoned by her thoughts, he entered the room.

"Care to tell me why you decided to have your eyes examined?" he asked, picking up his coffee and joining her on the sofa.

"You want an honest answer?" she replied, keeping her eyes closed.

"Only if it flatters my ego," Charles answered with a soft chuckle. "If tact requires that you lie, then do me a favor and change the subject."

Johanna's eyelids opened slowly. "I wanted to see you." She paused, deciding how to word a half-truth, a little white lie. . . . "To find out if reality is as pleasurable as fantasy."

"And?" he prodded, sipping his hot beverage.

"Reality is better," she answered calmly, leveling her eyes directly into his, a flirting technique she had recently read about in *Cosmo.*

Setting his cup back on the coffee table, he laced his fingers through Johanna's. Turning her palm toward him, Charles kissed each finger.

"How real is reality?" he questioned between kisses, probing deeper into her hidden meaning. He unlaced his fingers and traced his tongue over her love line. "Real enough for you to accept that what I'm beginning to feel for you goes beyond being an old boyfriend?"

"Yes," she answered pensively. "But there are things in my past"—she lifted her eyes to his bright, searching gaze—"and your past, that distort reality."

"Such as?" he queried, stroking her wavy bangs back from her forehead and planting a kiss on the slight widow's peak that made her face appear heart-shaped.

"Such as my reasons for marrying Bill."

Momentarily she wondered if she should tell him the whole truth. He didn't have to understand her past to play a temporary part in her future. Did she secretly want him to feel guilty about running off with Susan? Was this an attempt to purge her own soul, or his? She couldn't answer her own questions. She simply knew it was time to tell him how devastated she had been.

"When you married Susan I felt as though the sun had been ripped from the sky. I'd loved you for years and years." Johanna lowered her head and confessed, "I married the first man I could find who outwardly resembled you."

His shoulders hunched as though she had hit him squarely in the chest. Giving a light squeeze to her fingertips, he gently dropped her hand back to her lap.

"I married Susan because she told me she was pregnant," he explained, choosing each word carefully. "She was really only a sexual stand-in for you. As it turned out, I fell for the oldest line woman has ever spun. She wasn't pregnant." He laughed harshly, then disclosed, "She didn't even want children! She died . . . with one of her lovers in a car accident." His hand raked through his hair as his voice dropped an octave. "I vowed at the graveyard I'd never marry again."

"I made the same vow outside the courthouse," Johanna empathized. She knew how he felt—betrayed, torn apart, disgusted with himself.

"That's reality. Since her death I've settled for romantic fantasy. Only one letter changes 'living together' into 'loving together.' The single letter *I* makes the difference."

Silence, deep as a freshwater well, sprung between them. Johanna wished the hands of time could be moved back, then shook her head, retracting the wish. Nothing would have changed. In her childish naiveté, she would still be saying, "No, Chuck," and he would have found another willing partner. Fate wouldn't allow any variation in the outcome.

"I didn't seek you out looking for a husband, Charles. Nor am I looking for a roommate," she added, seeing the fire blaze beneath the blue surface of his eyes.

"Then what are the ground rules, hon?" One curved finger lifted her pointed chin until it was tilted up toward his lips.

Dodge the question, her mind urged. *He isn't ready for the whole truth. Don't take a chance on being rejected!*

Her dark eyes darted from left to right, trying to avoid his piercing appraisal. The finger holding her chin immobile tightened slightly. The firm pressure brought her gaze back to his.

"I'd like to get to know you better before I answer that question," she responded shakily.

The nearness of his lean frame radiated heat; his eyes glistened with hunger. Charles brushed her lips gently with the fleshy part of his thumb. She knew he had disclosed a part of himself he had kept hidden from others. He'd trusted her with his darkest secret; she had done the same.

As though to wipe away the mutual sorrow, he replaced his thumb with his lips. Coaxingly, tenderly, they moved from one corner of her mouth to the other. The tips of his fingers nestled into the soft, dark curls at her temples as his hands framed her face.

Lazily her eyelids closed. The gentleness of the kisses and the clean smell of soap and aftershave filled her senses. Tilting her head back, she exposed the long, slender expanse of throat leading to the satin smoothness of her caftan. The pulse at the base of her throat beat steadily until his moist lips touched the fluttering, pulsating hollow, then accelerated.

The slow, undemanding pace suited Johanna. The silent lips told her he wouldn't demand anything she withheld. The sigh she heard when her arms circled his neck was one of contentment. They had shared the failures in their lives, shared the agonizing defeat their spouses had dealt them, and now they shared the joy of shattering the pain that had encompassed them both.

Johanna shifted her body toward Charles and in one smooth movement found herself brought across his lap and held closely.

"From this moment on, the past is wiped away," Charles whispered. "We're a man and a woman attracted to each other, not bound by the rules of yesteryear."

His hand slipped between their clothing. One by one, without haste, he released the tiny buttons decorating the front of her caftan. Johanna watched as a smile flickered across his face. The front of her gown gaped to the waist with only a sheer, lacy bra covering her breasts. His fingertips touched the taut mounds above the lacy edge, and she knew he was waiting for the proverbial, "No, Chuck." He cupped the fullness, lowering his head to the cleavage. Inhaling deeply, he murmured, "Your skin is soft . . . delicious."

The roughness of his tongue stroked the exposed skin. His mouth moved over the lace, nipping, circling, then blowing hot warmth through the scanty fabric. The anticipation of feeling his mouth, unrestricted by clothing, sent a shaft of pleasure from her sensitized breasts downward. Almost of their own will, her arms enfolded his head more closely as he moved from one breast to the other, leaving a trail of fire blazing behind the sweet heat.

Charles's head rose. Her heavy-lidded gaze revealed the fire he had started by his gentle persuasion. Parting her lips, she invited a deeply passionate kiss.

"Unfasten it for me, honey," he crooned before sucking lightly at the bow of her lower lip. "Now," he urged.

Just as she freed her breasts from the restraining garment, his tongue slipped urgently into the honeyed sweetness of her mouth. The

41

double sensation of tongue and hand, rotating, kneading, exploring, sent the blood coursing through her veins, contrasting sharply with the slow, provocative pace of his lovemaking.

The roughness of his hands peaked each crest as she, hands trembling, unfastened his shirt, tugging at the shirttail to remove it from his beltless pants, then pulling the sleeves away, one at a time.

Flesh against flesh, unyielding muscle against malleable softness, roughness against smoothness, they molded their torsos together, fusing, separating, fusing again. Johanna couldn't get close enough; she moved side to side, relishing the feel of their intimately touching skin. The low groan she heard could have come from deep in her throat, or Charles's. She didn't know . . . or care.

Breathing in short pants, she didn't object when the silky caftan was lowered, the bra completely removed and flung aside. She wantonly arched upward, allowing him to completely undress her until only the satin strip of her bikini panties covered her slender form.

"I didn't remember how lovely you were, Johanna. More beautiful in reality than in fantasy."

Without haste, he lowered her until they both lay in the deep cushions, pressed together, shoulder to thigh. Charles stroked from breast to waist to upper thigh. Her cheek pressed against his upper arm, and she felt his muscle bulge then lengthen with each stroke. Her entire mindless being was focused on the masterly hands that molded, stroked, rubbed, caressed . . . evoking a passionate desire to be a part of this man, her first love. She wanted to bring the past forward and make it their future.

There had been no passion in her life for years. How had she survived in that emotional desert? She was starved for love, but now, as Charles traced erotic paths, discovering the inches of skin that brought the most response, she realized she was in danger of letting a decade of desire destroy her carefully laid plans.

Mentally she recited the litany that had become her driving force in life: *I want a child. I want a child, not a husband, not a lover, only . . . only a child.*

"What's wrong?" Charles asked hoarsely. "Did the alarm finally ring?" His lips recaptured her mouth, drawing her breath into his body as though by doing so he could replenish it with his own fiery heat. His desire was evident as he drew her hips against him. "It's too late, Johanna. God, Johanna, what do you want if not this?" he muttered against her throat as he hooked his thumb at the waistband of her panties, pulling them below her knees, then casting them aside as they slipped off her slender legs.

"I want you . . ." Johanna mumbled into the crispness of his hair, "to give me a child."

CHAPTER THREE

Splashing icy water over his bare back would have had the same effect as her revelation. Charles shuddered before drawing away. Propping himself on one elbow, he swept penetrating eyes over her face.

"That's why I came to your office," she explained, struggling to get a grip on her own passion-fraught limbs.

In a single fluid motion, he was off the sofa, standing, hands on hips in front of her. "Is this a woman libber's way of proposing marriage?" he asked, grinding the question out between clenched teeth.

Easing herself upright, Johanna felt defenseless sitting naked in front of him. Seeing her discomfort, Charles picked up her caftan from the floor and tossed it on the cushion beside her bare legs.

"No," she answered bluntly, gathering her wits to logically persuade Charles to understand her situation.

He stood as though his feet were planted in concrete, his eyes narrowed, watching as she slipped into the clinging fabric, pulled it over her head, then nervously fumbled with the buttons, which stubbornly refused to go into the small openings.

I've botched it, she thought, an acidic taste filling her mouth. The heat of passion was absolutely the worst time to mention babies. Especially since she now knew he had been trapped into a faithless marriage by the same word: baby. She had to clear up the misunderstanding before he left in complete disgust.

"If not marriage, what do you want?"

"A baby of my own," she answered, stating the complex issue simply. She watched Charles collapse into an armchair, bewilderment etching lines on his brow.

"I don't think you've thought through this thoroughly . . ." he began, but Johanna interrupted.

"I have! I've always wanted children. I'm

thirty-four years old, have plenty of money in the bank, and I've resigned from teaching. When I become pregnant, I'll move out of state, have the baby, and make up some story about being a widow."

As rapidly as possible, she disclosed her plans, not allowing any pauses or breaks in her explanation. Closing the last button on her gown, she glanced up to see his reaction. His mouth literally hung open.

"You've made me a father and a corpse in one mouthful. Thanks!" he yelled in shock, clenching one hand tightly on the arm of the chair and leaning toward Johanna.

"Don't be ridiculous. I'm not asking for commitment or even love . . . just a baby." She flashed him a broad smile, hoping he would see the logic of her plan.

"Well, I'll be. Prim and proper Johanna Jenkins *wants* to be an unmarried mother with *me* providing stud service," he exclaimed. He shook his head negatively as though he couldn't believe his ears.

"Crudely put, but accurate," Johanna responded, brushing her tousled hair back from her face with both hands. "Are you willing?"

Charles threw back his head and laughed. Rising to his feet he taunted, "You won't respect me tomorrow if I let you have your way with me tonight." There was no mirth in his eyes or in the stiff manner in which he braced his arms against his sides.

"A direct quote from the past? I recall saying it," she acknowledged, "but that was long ago. I've changed; you've changed; society has changed. If I didn't respect you, I wouldn't have chosen you."

Two long strides brought him toe-to-toe with Johanna. "Now, let me see if I have the complete picture." Bending down so their eyes were level, he began, "I impregnate you, then merrily go on my way. No ties. No responsibilities. No emotional involvement."

Unwavering, her eyes glued themselves to his. This was the moment of truth. Nodding her head she answered softly, "That's correct."

"Is tonight the night?" he asked pointedly.

"As a matter of fact, it is," she responded. A flush crept from her neck and spread over her high cheekbones.

"I'll be . . ." he muttered, touching her fiery cheek. "You're serious. Why didn't you just let my desire for you take its normal course? You know I'd have made love to you."

"I lived one lie for fourteen years. Only a fool makes the same mistakes over and over. You didn't hide what you wanted, to live with me, so

I felt as though I had to be as honest with you as you were with me."

"You can justify having my baby but not living with me?" he mumbled, putting one hand over the clenched fist on her lap. "That is one piece of feminine logic beyond me. It doesn't make sense!"

"The baby won't be *our* child if I assume responsibility from the very beginning. You'll never see it. As you so aptly put it, you can merrily go on your way."

One child, one parent, bonded by mutual love and need, made a reasonable equation in Johanna's mind. And with Charles being the father, the baby would be the equivalent to a miracle in her life.

"Why me?" he asked, then, as though her reasoning had suddenly dawned upon him, he added, "First love?"

Johanna nodded.

Drawing a deep breath Charles arose, moving toward the alcove containing a small built-in bar.

"I need a drink. Want one?"

"Wine would be fine." Turning, she watched as he removed a wineglass and highball glass from the display shelf. Deftly he pulled the Chivas Regal off another shelf and poured a liberal shot into the squat glass. His other hand reached into the ice bucket, extracting a handful of ice cubes, and clinked them into the half-full glass of amber-colored liquid. He stooped, opened the small refrigerator below the counter, and asked, "Red or white?"

"White, please."

Still languid from their loving, Johanna slowly pushed herself off the sofa. The tips of her breasts, still erect, showed through the satin softness of her gown. Trying to appear unconscious of her body's betrayal, she crossed to the bar stool. The pendulant swaying, unrestricted by the bra she normally wore, added to the sensuality of the satin gently caressing her bare skin.

"You don't need one," Charles stated perceptively. "You never did. Don't be embarrassed, men have similar obvious problems." The cheeky grin made his dimples deepen. "That's why I'm *behind* the bar."

Handing to her the wine he had already poured, Charles intentionally let the back of his hand rake against the visible proof of her desire, saying, "You're some woman."

Johanna closed her eyes, recalling his recent fondling, which made her squirm in her chair as she realized how much she wanted to continue what they had begun. Dark eyes opening a fraction of an inch, she quietly asked, "Will you make love to me?"

"No, not tonight," he answered softly.

Her shoulders slumped in defeat. Charles had rejected her offer. Lifting the delicate stemware, she gulped down half of the contents.

"That is, unless we take precautions," he added when he saw the despondent reaction his refusal brought. "I'd gladly rip that piece of froth off your body and make mad, passionate love to you in the middle of the floor—but not if fertilizing an egg is the primary goal. I'm not available for stud services."

He raised his hand to stop Johanna from protesting. "That is the only way I perceive this. I concede to your female logic, but you eliminated the male viewpoint." His index finger remained in her vision. "Number one, how do I know you'll be a good mother? Number two"—the middle finger joined the index finger—"what if I decide I want to share the raising of a child? And for the third and final factor"—the ring finger rose—"if you can accept being an unmarried mother, why not a live-in arrangement?" The three fingers lowered and stroked her tanned arm, from wrist to elbow, which was propped on the sleek wooden bar. "Think about my side of the . . . bed."

Johanna pondered his objections thoughtfully, twirling the stem of the glass in her hand. "Perhaps a stranger would be better," she uttered, lowering her forehead into both hands.

The thought of approaching a strange man was repugnant. How could she proposition a stranger?

The words had barely slipped past her lips when she felt Charles's hands clamped on the softness of her upper arms. The sharp shake she received toppled her head from her hands.

"No way! That would be dangerous—you don't know what you might get yourself into." He spat angrily. Exasperated, he dropped her arms as though they burned his hands, picked up his drink, and tossed the remaining Scotch to the back of his throat.

"You're not responsible, so don't worry about it. Okay?"

"Dammit, Johanna, you are about to do something stupid!" He punctuated his belief by slamming his glass on the bar top.

Swiveling off the bar stool, Johanna walked to the chair where his jacket lay draped over the tall back. She'd been called stupid throughout her marriage and didn't need another male putting her down.

"Thank you for coming to dinner," she politely tossed over her shoulder. "I've enjoyed having you."

"And I'd enjoy having you," he replied, twisting her words, "but not tonight."

Picking the jacket up, stroking the fabric, Johanna muttered to herself, "Not any night." More loudly, crisply, she spoke to Charles, "I'd appreciate your leaving now."

Charles's hands clapped together twice in mocking salute. "Class dismissed? Spoken like a true schoolmarm." His hands applauded again. "Great performance but it won't wash. I'm not leaving until you promise not to do anything dumb."

Wanting to wound his ego, she pivoted and, using woman's age-old excuse for not making love, said, "Sorry about your headache."

"Oh, hon, more than my head aches," he quipped, "but I'm not going anywhere until you give me your word you won't do anything foolish."

"Now you listen to me, and you listen good," she said ungrammatically. "I'm not stupid and I'm not a fool. Men!" she scoffed, slapping her hand against her silken-clad thigh disparagingly. "When a woman finds a solution to a problem that is in conflict with a *male* solution, she automatically becomes stupid and foolish . . . dumb. Well, pardon me for living! Just get the hell out of here!" Wadding his jacket into a tight, cumbersome ball, she flung it with all her

53

strength at his shoulders. Her aim fell below its intended mark, hitting Charles below the belt.

"I'm sorry," she muttered almost instantly, feeling utterly ashamed of her untypical behavior.

"*If* you're truly sorry, I'll forgive you on one condition: Promise you won't do anything rash."

Reaching down, Johanna picked the jacket off the floor and shook the wrinkles out. She needed to plan an alternative course, anyway. The goal hadn't changed . . . it'd only been postponed.

"I promise," she vowed sincerely.

Silently, he lifted his jacket from her hands and headed toward the door. Johanna followed in his footsteps. When he abruptly stopped, she bumped into his back.

"Sorry," she mumbled, hands on his waist, pushing herself backward and to his side. The situation was awkward enough without her rounding it out by being clumsy also. Staring at her toes to keep from facing him, she silently chastised herself for revealing the purpose of her intimate dinner too soon. Impetuosity had always been a flaw in her character. When would she learn that the old adage "patience is a virtue" was true?

The hairs at the nape of her neck tingled as Charles's hand swept over them. Threading the loose locks through his long fingers, he tugged gently, raising her head.

The dimple she loved flashed as a smile quirked his lips upward. "I still want to make love to you . . . never doubt that fact."

The firm hold at the nape of her neck was the only thing that kept Johanna from lowering her head. She felt herself being propelled against the broad expanse of his chest and her soft curls being tucked under his chin.

"He who fights and runs away lives to fight another day." The singsong limerick was followed by a hug and a brief kiss on the top of her head. "I'll call you tomorrow."

Silently, she nodded her head in agreement. Without another word, Charles opened the door and walked out, closing it quietly behind himself.

Zombielike, Johanna flicked off the lights and climbed the steps to her solitary bedroom. The emotional roller coaster had drained her of all energy. Scarlett O'Hara's famous line, "I'll think about it tomorrow," was the only coherent thought that spun through her muddled brain. Plan A had failed. Did she have enough courage to follow Plan B?

CHAPTER FOUR

The picture, torn, taped, and worn, had it been able to speak, could have told a story of vitriolic rage. Once when his wife had discovered it tucked away among business cards in his billfold, she had tried to shred the innocent beauty the picture held. Putting the pieces back together had been more important to Charles than pacifying the woman he had married but never loved.

Charles sighed, raking his fingers through his dark, straight hair. She's beautiful, he thought. Strong, courageous, determined . . . crazy! Chuckling to himself, he returned the once-mu-

picture back to the dark recesses of his

Johanna had paid him the ultimate in compliments—she wanted to have his child—then slapped him down by not wanting to be emotionally involved. Groaning, he leaned back in the desk chair. Deep down, at gut level, he knew the love they had shared had not died. The picture he had carried in his breast pocket, next to his heart, testified to that fact.

When she had walked through the office door, he had busied his hands with the wide array of optometry tools spread on the tray in front of the examination chair to keep himself from involuntarily pulling her into his arms. Touching the softness of her face as he conducted the examination had been an exquisite exercise in self-control. The darkness of the room, fortunately, hid the physical longing that he knew was rigidly evident.

Bright blue eyes closed as he remembered the touch, taste, and feel of Johanna. His loins tightened as the memory became more explicit. He swallowed to dislodge the lump in his throat. Estee Lauder, the aphrodisiac she wore, drifted into his senses. The index finger on his left hand crossed the fleshy mound below his thumb as he recalled his lips trailing between the firm mounds of her breasts.

"Doctor, are you awake?"

Damn!

"Yes, Betty . . . just checking my eyelids out for holes!"

"Find any this time?" Betty, his elderly receptionist, asked, chuckling at the joke they shared every time she caught him napping.

Bringing the office chair back into its erect position, he asked, "Have you changed your perfume? That's pretty racy stuff I'm smelling."

"Estee Lauder. Harold gave it to me for our fortieth anniversary last week. He's trying to put some zing in his zinger." Betty released the folders she held next to her ample bosom and arranged them neatly on her boss's desk. "Stuff works, too," she added with a merry twinkle in her vivid gray eyes.

Charles glanced up at the wrinkled, rotund woman who had worked for him for years. He knew he was the son she had never had. Three girls, grown and married, had made Betty a grandmother, but he also knew Betty had a special place in her generous heart that was reserved for him.

"You're not going to ask for maternity leave, are you?" he joked, playfully swatting her on the rump.

Betty tousled his hair as she would a small child's. "I'll leave baby-making up to you. I just do it for fun." Turning toward the door, chuckling, she stopped midway. "Oh, yes, I almost forgot. First thing this morning, Johanna Jenkins phoned. Said she had changed her mind and wouldn't be needing contacts after all and to thank you for everything."

Frantically grabbing the phone, he didn't hear Betty tell him that his only remaining morning appointment had cancelled. Punching a series of numbers into the phone, he didn't see the perplexed look on her face as she quietly closed the door and left his office.

The strident ringing of the phone interrupted Johanna's packing. A tear splashed on the green vinyl suitcase as she snapped the fasteners into place. Automatically she reached over to the nighttable and picked up the phone.

"Johanna?"

Stunned, she didn't reply.

"Johanna. Don't hang up!"

Hearing the command, she delayed the motion of returning the receiver to its base.

"Charles? Didn't you get the message I left?"

"Message received. You promised not to do anything until I made a decision."

The accusing tone in his voice raised Johanna's hackles. She had made no such promise. *Well*, she admitted as her conscience reared its head, *not exactly*.

"I promised not to do anything rash. I'm not," she answered defensively, sinking onto the bed beside her packed suitcase.

"You're splitting hairs. You know the intent of the promise. I'll bet your bags are packed and you're ready to find another father for your baby, aren't you?"

Half right, half wrong, she thought, wishing he didn't know her as well as he did.

"As a matter of fact, they are, but I had planned on going to the farm this weekend *before* I had dinner with you," she lied, trying to throw him off track.

"Were you planning on taking me with you?" he questioned.

"No."

"Had we made babies all night, you'd have calmly crawled out of my arms, left the bed, and gone to Southeast Missouri? Even your logic isn't that twisted."

Johanna felt the fluttering of butterfly wings in her stomach at the mention of Plan A. She had tried and failed. There was no point in arguing with Charles over what could have happened; it hadn't.

"No comment," she answered tersely.

"Well, it just so happens my need to get away from St. Louis coincides with your need for fresh farm air," he said, inviting himself along.

"The farmhouse has one bedroom," she pointedly replied.

"The sleeping arrangements can be negotiated on the trip down there. I'll pick you up in fifteen minutes; we'll swing by my place, then head toward the Bootheel."

The line was disconnected before she had a chance to argue.

"Of all the arrogant, dictatorial . . ." she sputtered, slamming the phone down. As she shook one finger in its direction, her anger grew. "You don't have the right to negotiate *anything* with me," she shouted. She reached for her suitcase, ready to flee, when the incongruity of the statement made her pause. Logic told her she had given him that right the previous evening. A strong sense of fairness made her release the grip and scurry into the bathroom.

The mirror reflected a night of soul-searching, tossing and turning. A cold shower hadn't relieved the ache that had awakened her during the early hours. The stinging spray had made further sleep impossible. She had paced the floor for hours and finally decided the peace and tranquillity of the farm would be a more soothing environment to rehash her thinking.

Bruiselike smudges beneath her eyes emphasized their luminous quality. A light coat of moisturizer and makeup did little to hide her sleepless night. Adding a trace of blusher and mascara added artificial color and depth to the one-dimensional base coat.

"When he gets here I'll tell him I'm going there for peace and quiet," she coached herself. She popped the lid off her lipstick, deftly stroking the light crimson color over her lips.

Hopeless, she mouthed as her curly hair refused to straighten into orderly waves. "Why couldn't I have long straight hair like Rosmund," she muttered. Her sister's hair was gorgeous.

An unbidden insight flashed across her mind. Were there other things about Rosmund she envied? Had the baby Rosmund recently had subconsciously brought about the maternal urges Johanna was experiencing? Admitting the possible connection, she recalled holding the infant as it squirmed, lips nuzzling her breast. Rosmund had taken the child and modestly covered her shoulder with a towel and nursed the infant, and Johanna had felt so inadequate.

The incessant ringing of the door bell brought Johanna's thoughts back to her present predicament. *Be firm,* she lectured herself silently, running down the steps to the entry way. *Don't let anyone make decisions for you.*

She flung the door open wide and was immediately swept into Charles's strong arms. "God, I couldn't get here fast enough," he muttered into the crook of her neck.

The lecture she had given herself was immediately forgotten as his arms tightened. Johanna wrapped her arms around his waist, flattening herself against his length. His hug made tears collect behind her eyes; their saltiness soothing the scratchiness earlier tears had caused.

"Unless you want the neighbors to see an X-rated love scene, I suggest we shut the door," Charles huskily teased.

"X-rated?" she repeated. "Does that mean you've changed your mind?"

Tucking her securely under his arm, Charles closed the door before answering with a question. "Have you changed your *mind* or in this case, *man?*" he teased, dropping a kiss on the riot of curls beneath his chin. Side by side, he led her into the living room. "Don't answer. You'll deflate my near-forty ego. I've come up with a compromise. Sit down," he instructed, pointing to the sofa, "don't interrupt, and we'll discuss the options rationally."

Johanna watched the teasing light that had crinkled the corners of his eyes leave as the seriousness of the last phrase left his mouth. Sinking into the softness of the leather cushions, she watched Charles start to seat himself beside her, then move to the chair opposite the sofa.

"Well?" she asked when he had settled into the wing chair. His eyes were devouring the snug fabric of her worn jeans, which tightly encased her slender legs, and the deep scoop of the stretch tank top. Without looking down, she felt a physical reaction to his penetrating stare and willed the tips of her breasts to relax as she saw his knowing fingers rub the armrest, then clench and unclench.

"Stop it, Charles. You're embarrassing me."

Crossing his legs, ankle over knee, he jested, "I'm about to embarrass myself also."

Electricity shot from the sofa to the armchair. Their minds met and mingled in the silence. Johanna wanted to eliminate the space, crawl up on his lap, and feel his lips caress every square inch of her skin. Shaking her head negatively, she cleared it of the erotic fantasy.

Charles sensed her desire and the rejection of the dream. Interlacing his fingers, he placed them on his lap. She had to understand his feelings before they could advance any further.

"I'm going to give you a sample of male logic. *A,* you want a baby without a father; *b,* I want a wife without benefit of marriage. *Solution? A* lives with *b,* which will result in *c,* a child. What do you think?"

Johanna bit her lower lip thoughtfully as she contemplated his compromise. Her plan hadn't included cohabitation for a reason she didn't care to discuss with anyone. A clinical coupling at the right time of the month was the only thing she could handle. Scornfully, she knew Charles wouldn't be around next month to keep his end of the bargain when he found that out. Her stomach muscles twisting, she wondered if she could manipulate his offer? Live with him but not share a bed until the time of conception was right? Then the humiliation of his knowing would be forgotten. He'd *willingly* leave after one night in her bed. Nobody wants a lousy lover, she disparaged, knowing the fire he would build would freeze before the final culmination. It always had.

Charles, watching the woman he had always loved gnawing at her lip, eyes filling with pain, was frustrated. What had happened to his lovely Johanna? Her mental anguish was readily apparent. Charles winced.

Was living with him that distasteful? The physical attraction was there; he would have known if she found him physically repugnant. *She responds even when we're not touching!* Maybe, like Suzy, he thought, she responds to all men. *Not again,* he pleaded, *oh, God, don't let that happen to me again.*

Tormented by the possibility, Charles stood, the thought driving him to action. "Let's try it for the weekend. Nothing permanent. No commitment. No sex."

Johanna couldn't see the bleakness marring his face. The long silence had communicated her doubts, which made the tentative rejection she had been forming in the back of her mind unnecessary. The new offer held greater appeal. She wouldn't be forced to expose her failure as a woman. They could enjoy the companionship they had had years ago without complications.

"I'd love it," she said joyously.

Charles turned, a wide smile replacing the frown. Johanna was his, at least for the weekend. "Come on, woman. Get your suitcase. Time's a wasting." Crossing to the telephone as she bounced up the steps two at a time, he called the office and told Betty not to expect him until Monday.

"Hot date?" Betty inquired, smothering a laugh unsuccessfully.

"The hottest, Madame Cupid," he replied. "Hold down the optical fort until I return."

"Aye, aye, captain. By the way, I placed an order for Johanna's contacts. They'll be here Tuesday. Would you tell her to schedule an appointment?"

"And what makes you so certain I'll see Johanna?" Charles queried.

"She wears Estee Lauder . . . works every time," Betty replied perkily.

"Mrs. Betty Atkinson, do you know the meaning of insubordinate?" he asked in a boss-threatening-employee tone.

"Not in my vocabulary, doctor, but I do know the meaning of horny. *Webster's Dictionary* defines it as . . ." Her chuckles were the last thing Charles heard as he lowered the receiver.

Betty was definitely the type of grandmother who performed on *Saturday Night Live.* Funny, he mused, she had not liked the other women he had filled his life with. This time her endorsement couldn't have been louder.

Jingling the change in his pocket, Charles waited impatiently. "Two minutes, Johanna, then I'm coming up there," he shouted from the landing on the steps.

"I'm coming," drifted downward, accompanied by a melodic laugh.

"And I'm breathing hard," he muttered. He seriously doubted he would be able to hold true to his hands-off promise, but he'd try. "Probably die trying," he muttered under his breath.

An hour later, two suitcases in the trunk of his Eldorado, they headed south.

"Do you lease the farm?" Charles asked,

breaking the deep thoughts Johanna contemplated.

"I have to. Genetically, my grandparents kept their green thumbs. I can't grow garden vegetables much less wheat, corn, and milo," she scoffed.

"I can," Charles said, weaving a thread into the pattern of her life. Glancing at her relaxed form, which was pressed against the door, he playfully tugged at her bare arm. "Come closer and I'll reveal all my deep, dark gardening secrets."

Laughing, she scooted across the plush velour to the center of the seat. His arm casually looped over her shoulders, which made his hand dangle dangerously near her breast. Johanna restrained the physical urge to lean forward and feel a more intimate touch than the friendly arm-across-shoulder contact.

Strange, she mused, her mind flitting back into the past. Sitting next to Bill had never lessened the gap between them. The world and its wars could have filled the space with plenty of room left over. Why did she feel this close affinity with Charles? Eyes searching his face, she wondered if maybe, just maybe, the missing ingredient in making love with Bill had been a total lack of friendship, and it would be there with Charles. Could the bond of friendship be the secret of glorious lovemaking? Once and for all, would the self-doubts about her sexuality be wiped away? Or would the disappointment if she failed be increased tenfold?

Johanna's shoulders hunched. It would be a fatal blow to her self-esteem should sharing a bed with Charles be as sterile an experience as what she had had with Bill. Momentarily she wished she had let honesty fly with the summer breeze last night and found out the answers to her questions. If it was different with Charles, she would no longer have to deal with the recriminations Bill had harped on; the divorce would have been completely due to his infidelities and not her frigidity.

Forearm resting on Charles's thigh, Johanna squeezed his kneecap lightly and grinned up into his smiling face. "Tell me your gardening secrets," she requested, preferring to hear the sound of his voice rather than listen to her own thoughts.

"It's strictly a matter of fertilization. Plants starve to death when they aren't fed."

Was the wink he flashed indicating a comparison between plants and women? she wondered, knowing his penchant for meaningful undertones.

"Of course," he continued, "they need the right amount of exposure to the sun also. You can't stick them in a closet and expect them to survive."

"My houseplants thrive on water, good music, and my talking to them," Johanna retorted smugly, proud of the lush ferns and philodendrons in her home.

"Some plants are tough and can withstand loving neglect, but any food-bearing plant needs sustenance."

"Are you comparing childbearing with producing food?" she asked pointedly.

Charles suppressed a smile. *The lady is sharp enough to see through the manure I was spreading.*

"There does appear to be a similarity in nature's design," he quipped, smoothing the faded denim over her thigh and patting it gently. Cocking one eyebrow, keeping his eyes on the four-lane highway, he asked, "Are water and talk enough for you?"

"Flattery in the morning isn't your forte, is it? Being compared to a stalk of corn or wheat lacks glamour! Tell me, Farmer Franklin, shall I spray myself with fish emulsion when we stop for lunch?"

Chuckling, his fingers tweaked a stray tendril of hair by her cheek. "My receptionist approves of your fragrance," he teased. "Says it puts zing in her husband's zinger."

70

Clearing her throat to cover up an impending outburst of laughter, Johanna asked, "Does perfume affect you the same way?"

"It's better than fish emulsion," he answered, casting her a wide grin and another wink.

"Was that an attempt to get back in my good graces? First you compare me with a stalk of corn, and now you compliment my choice of fragrance." She snorted disparagingly, rapping his knee lightly.

Johanna watched as his eyes widened in mock horror. "You must have misunderstood. Never would I compare your beauty to a stalk with several sets of ears." His finger circled the outer shell of her ear, flicking the small, dangling loop hanging from it. "Humans poke holes in their ears to increase their beauty . . . no self-respecting ear of corn would consider such a travesty."

Johanna laughed. "If nature had provided women with corn-silk decorations, we wouldn't, either," she retorted, justifying her pierced ears. "Men are every bit as vain as women. How many *men* are wearing contacts rather than glasses?"

"Exactly my point. More women than men wear contacts, and incidentally, yours are on order."

"Vanity was not the motivation behind my

appointment," she said, huskily tracing the knife-sharp crease of his dark slacks from knee to mid-thigh.

"Your reason kept me on my feet pacing the floor half the night," he confessed, the teasing light leaving his sky-bright eyes.

"Me, too," she responded softly, following the crease back to his knee.

"Tired?"

Charles's question was graphically answered by a jaw-popping yawn, which she politely hid behind her hand. Eyes watering, she wiped the corners with the tip of her ring finger.

"I seem to recall your falling asleep before the back wheels were out of your parents' driveway. You're struggling to stay awake now, aren't you?"

"Mmmmm," she responded, leaning her head back against his arm and closing her eyes. "My parents trained Rosmund and me to sleep rather than torment each other in the backseat. Bill hated traveling with me, said the radio was better company."

A frown wrinkled her forehead. Why in the world had she revealed that tidbit of information? Usually she kept the bitterness and mini-failures behind closed doors carefully marked "Private, no trespassing." No one, Charles included, wanted to hear about the thorough job of character assassination she had undergone during her marriage. The understanding friendliness Charles exuded was destroying her decision to keep quiet about personal problems.

"Take a catnap," Charles encouraged, smoothing her brow and cradling her head against his shoulder. "Silence between us is better than the inane chatter most couples indulge in."

As she sat cuddled against him, the protective feelings he had always felt toward Johanna surfaced. She wouldn't openly admit it, but he knew she had been hurt—badly hurt—by the failure of her marriage. Analyzing the minute amount she had let slip, he wondered about their marriage. The cryptic remark she made regarding hearing about their wedding night all the way to the divorce court bothered him. If he had stayed out of Susan's willing arms, initiating Johanna into the rites of love would have been his privilege.

Drawing her closer, he heard the slow, even pace of her breathing. He was puzzled by the entire situation. There was more to Johanna wanting a child than she had told him. What force was driving her toward wanting to be an unmarried mother? Reliving the conversation of the previous evening over and over had not given him the key to the mystery. He seemed to get hung up each time he reached the part where she had mentioned picking up a strange man.

Am I jealous? Charles shook his head. She wouldn't be desperate enough to actually take such a drastic step, he thought, reassuring himself. Rationally, he knew he couldn't allow it to happen but realized he had little influence over her decision.

In the wee hours of the morning, he had narrowed his choices down to two. He could fulfill his wildest dreams by making love to Johanna, knowing she would walk out of his life when her goal was reached, or he could refuse her offer and worry about who was in her bed. Either way he would lose.

There had to be a more mutually agreeable solution. Why had she summarily dismissed living with him? Why? Didn't Johanna realize that loving her once was as impossible as eating one potato chip or taking one lick off a double-dip ice cream cone? Stomach growling, he smiled at his own discovery. Johanna was as necessary to him as food.

"Marriage?" he mumbled aloud.

She had denied it, but could she possibly be steering him toward the church aisle? Eyes narrowing, he scrutinized the thought. Had she substituted fatherhood as the payoff for sleeping together in the place of virginity?

Sex was a ploy women habitually used to make men come around to their viewpoint. *Humph!* he silently snorted in distaste. *I've been duped once . . . a hard lesson, not to be forgotten.* Avoiding that particular trap had become second nature to him. No woman, Johanna included, was going to make a fool of him again. Setting his jaw, thrusting it forward, he reaffirmed the vow he had made years ago: Marriage is out . . . never again.

The fresh smell of Johanna's hair filtering into his senses was a form of gentle seduction. I'm not about to succumb to gentle seduction, he mused, lips twisting cynically. Stroking the bare flesh on her arm, he relaxed. They had made an agreement and, by God, he wasn't going to be the one to break it . . . if he could help it.

CHAPTER FIVE

"We're here," Charles said, driving the car up the rutted lane to the old farmhouse. Gripping Johanna's sleeping form against him, he cushioned the jarring motion caused by the car hitting potholes. Braking, he asked, "Sweet dreams?"

Reluctantly she pushed away from the warm pillow his shoulder had made. Drowsily glancing in the rearview mirror she saw the red-tainted rosiness of the cheek that had lain against him. "The sweetest," she replied honestly, remembering the major role he had played in her dreams. "I didn't mean to sleep the entire drive," she apologized.

Hugging Johanna, he shrugged away the apology. "Let's stretch our legs before I carry our luggage in."

"*My* luggage . . . yours goes to the local Holiday Inn," she corrected, avoiding argument by sliding over and opening her car door. Once her feet were planted on the ground, a feeling of belonging, coming back to her roots, invigorated her.

Drowsiness, emotional conflicts, problematic decisions, belonged to someone other than Johanna, who stepped into the nearby field of soybeans and stooped, scooping sandy loam up into her hand and pressing its sunbaked warmth into the palm of her hand.

Silently Charles held out his hand toward her as he had on a visit so long ago. Johanna straightened and gave him the small clod of earth in her palm. Reliving the moment, he rolled the soil into a compact ball, then hurled it with a man's strength several rows away from them.

"I'm impressed," Johanna teased, bending, picking up another clod, and pitching it in the same direction. It fell short of his mark. "Last time I was closer."

Charles threaded his fingers between hers, bringing the back of her hand to his lips. "This time *we'll* be closer." The blue of his eyes, as clear as the sky above, promised to close the gap of years that had separated them.

"Want to go to the creek?" she asked. "We can hunt for arrowheads."

Nodding in agreement, a row of green leaves between their legs, they walked toward the gigantic cypress trees edging the slow-moving water bordering one side of the farm.

"I had the ones we found put in a glass case," Charles divulged. "They're in my study."

Grinning up at him, Johanna teased, "I seem to recall the stream being one of those places where my alarm system went defunct. Did you frame the bra, too?"

"That's a secret I refuse to divulge." Whacking her lightly on the rump, he challenged, "Beat me to the creek and I'll tell."

Not waiting for a reply, he dropped her hand and darted down the cultivated path. The sprint quickened when he glanced over his shoulder and saw Johanna hot on his heels. He lengthened his stride, and his loafers dug into the loose soil. Once before, she had claimed victory by pushing past him at the last moment, chucking one tennis shoe aside, and stepping into the shallow creek.

Scrambling through the undergrowth, he kicked off one loafer and sank his foot, sock and all, into the muddy bank.

"I win," he crowed, laughing boisterously.

Winded, Johanna plopped down, panting and giggling at the same time. Charles laughed as he stuck one finger under the ribbing of his muddy sock and whipped it off. Dunking his foot in the clear surface of the creek to remove the last traces of mud, he said lightly, "Now you owe me a kiss."

"Sorry. That wasn't the bet," she teased, breathing deeply, her lungs filling with air and the anticipation of having Charles kiss her as he had so many, many years ago. "You won the right to keep your secret."

Johanna reclined on the grass edging the bank; she invited the kiss, using her body rather than spoken words. She watched him remove his other sock, seeing the muscles across his back stretch, then relax. Unable to resist the temptation, she ran her hand up his spine, over the tautly stretched knit shirt.

"I excelled in track because of you. Every race, won or lost, ended with a kiss as a reward," he bargained lazily. Leaning back, rolling on his side, propping his head up with one hand, he hovered inches away from her mouth. Fingertips tracing the bow of her lower lip, he whispered, "Your kiss was a prize I cherished far more than the roomful of trophies I won."

She curled her slender arms around his neck.

Johanna brushed her closed lips against him and drew him over her.

"Oh, love . . . sweet love," he murmured, framing her face, searching for the secret she withheld. Did she want him as passionately as he wanted her? Did she need him for more than she'd bargained for? Her eyes widened, pulling him into their velvet depths. He inhaled sharply when the warmth of her hand crept beneath his shirt, heating the flesh on his back.

The magic touch of her other hand spread pleasurable sensations as it stroked through the short hair by his temple, to the longer locks at the crown of his head, down to the tapered length at the nape of his neck. Kissing the breath of air between them, she beckoned, offering an intimate kiss by barely parting her lips and moistening them with the tip of her tongue.

"Charles?"

The air, heated by the electric tension between them, crackled with seduction.

"Chuck," he whispered quietly. "Say it . . . mean it," he coaxed gently.

He had refused to accept the name she had used when she had kissed him, nearly loved him the other night. Knowing the significance of his request, Charles held his breath waiting for her decision.

Biting the soft inner lining of her lower lip,

she whispered, "Chuck," simultaneously praying that the fires spreading now from everywhere he touched her could thaw the "icicle maiden."

She heard and felt the breath he had held, and the low moan from the back of his throat, as their lips fused together. The probing tip of his tongue surged beyond the barriers of lips to drink thirstily from the well of long-denied passion. Her mind reeled with his name as he circled and swirled over her taste buds, scorching her with his fierce ardor.

Twisting and draping one leg over his thighs, Johanna tried to lose herself completely in their passion as his seeking hand nudged a space between her tank top and jeans. *This time, please,* she thought, *don't let anything stop the urgent fires. Don't let me tense up and ruin everything.*

She slowly kneaded the muscles in his back from spine to rib cage, then, when she reached his shoulders, she urgently increased the tempo of their loving. Charles shifted to his side, stringing a trace of kisses over her neck; his arms fiercely pressed the length of her body against his aroused masculine hardness. Male instinct brought her hips to his as his hands molded over her rounded buttocks.

Years of fantasies made his hands impatient to touch the feminine places denied to him as a young man. Pressing their torsos together with his left arm, he reached from spine to navel with his right hand quickly unsnapping, pushing her zipper down as his fingers surged impetuously, hastily, beneath her clothing to the most secret place of all.

Charles felt her stomach muscles tense at the swift invasion but was lost in the mindless passion of becoming one with Johanna, feeling himself sheathed in her softness. The kisses she had lavishly coated on his neck and face stopped.

"Need you . . . must . . . must," he muttered, capturing her full lower lip, nipping sharply when he felt her knees cross over his hand, forbidding entrance to the intimate part of her he avidly sought.

At that moment, he knew. Intent upon touch, his blind passion had ignored all sights and sounds. The noises coming from her throat were whimpers, not moans of passion. There were tears on her cheeks.

The rejection he felt swamped over his desire. The tension in his thighs dwindled to nothing but an acute ache. Flinging himself backward on the cool, damp earth, he felt Johanna roll away from him to her side, curling into a tight ball. Her tears were no longer silent but were sobs; deep, heart-rending sobs that violently shook her shoulders.

A tremor rushed through his body. Turbulent emotions racked his frame. Mentally he chastised himself for rushing through their lovemaking as though he were a randy sailor on leave. *In my dreams I was in control! Why not in reality? Oh, God, I've wanted, loved her for so damned long. Weak excuse! Why hadn't it been beautiful as I promised? It should have been! My fault, damn it. My fault!*

"My fault, honey. My fault," he murmured, rolling until their bodies fit together like two spoons. A tremor shaking his hand, he stroked her bare arm. She seemed unaware of his attempt to comfort her. Moisture gathered behind his own eyelids. Unmanly tears threatened to disgrace him further.

"Wasn't," he heard her gulp. "Mine . . . my fault. He was right. My God, all these years he was right." She covered her face with her hand, and the mixture of words and sobs became muffled and incoherent.

Puzzled, Charles tried to arrange the bits and pieces of information to make sense. Who was "he"? *Me? Why is she taking the blame for my mistake?*

"Failed . . . again," filtered through her fingertips.

Charles's bewilderment made him helpless. What could he do to ease the pain he had caused her? Cuddling her closer, he shushed the sobs, stroking damp tendrils of hair away from her face. Crying this long would make her physically ill.

"It's all right, love. Hush. Shhhhhh. It's okay," he whispered again and again, his voice crooning a comforting litany.

"Won't be. Never will be," she gasped in misery. "I'm sorry . . . sorry."

I'm a sorry excuse for a woman, she mentally berated herself. *Why?* After years of being married, being unsatisfied, being abused, why had she chanced this final humiliation? *It would have been better to have believed there was something wrong with Bill than to know . . . and now I know without a doubt . . . I'm the one responsible for our hideous honeymoon and all the years of nightly failure.*

The truth hurt unbearably. She had cherished the hope tucked away in the dark corners of her mind, that being loved by Charles would be different. She had desperately wanted it to be; she'd willed it to be but it wasn't.

Charles tried to turn her so he could see her face. She couldn't allow him to see how ravaged she felt. Her false dream had been stripped away. There was nothing but reality, and it was ugly, ugly, ugly. Too hideous for him to see or contemplate.

"No. Please, no," she begged, struggling in his arms. "Don't look at me." Sniffing, wiping the tears away with the backs of her hands, she tried to pull herself together.

"Johanna, I don't know what happened. What? Why?" Refusing to release her, he pleaded for an explanation, prayed for one that would exonerate him from the terrible mess his passion had created.

Heavily sighing, squeezing her eyes shut from her own pain, Johanna replied, "I'm frigid. In my ex-husband's precise description, I'm an icicle bitch. Don't blame yourself, Chuck."

"Has sex always left you cold?"

"I don't remember being on fire, desperately wanting him, but . . ." A flood of shame washed over her.

"But?" he encouraged softly.

"But with you I thought it would be different."

"You hoped the hunger we had for each other would burn through the ice," he uttered more to himself than to Johanna. He was beginning to understand. She wanted more than what she had originally told him. *Damn, I let her down because . . .*

"Don't feel sorry for me, Chuck. The problem isn't yours; it's mine."

"I rushed you. Had I been aware of what

you'd been through I think I would have been more sensitive to your needs and less preoccupied with mine. Oh, love, I've made a terrible mess of what should have been beautiful."

Johanna shook her head. Somehow, somewhere, hidden in her past there must be something her conscious mind hid, but she couldn't remember any disastrous encounters that would scar her like this. Ducking, using her arms to push away from Charles, she shook her head again and again.

Using his thumb and finger, he lifted her chin until their eyes met. "Is this baby issue related to the sex problem? Are you certain this isn't really a means of proving yourself as a woman?" he probed.

"I have an alternate plan, remember?" she replied, dodging the painful questions.

"What? Picking up some unsuspecting slob in a bar? Is that a viable solution?" he demanded harshly.

"Artificial insemination," she said, staring blindly into his clouded eyes.

"What?" he demanded in disbelief. "You're going to be bred like a—"

"Isn't that option better than the one *you* came up with?" Wrenching away, she sat up, drawing her knees to her chest. "The wonders of science have given women of the eighties options other than bar-bedding."

A fiery expletive burst through Charles's lips.

"My life . . . my failures . . . my solution," she stated flatly, drawing her knees closer to her chin.

"What happened here wasn't *your* failure!" he ground between clenched teeth, pulling one arm loose and making her face him. "Look at me!" he demanded. A mixture of anger and concern made his command hoarse. Seeing the misery in her dark eyes, his own anger fled. "Has this artificial insemination plan been in the back of your mind as the 'clinical,' no-commitment, no-father solution all along?"

"Yes," she replied truthfully. "Our making love was a last-ditch effort at not being a failure."

"Making love is a mutual success or a mutual failure," Charles reproached uncategorically.

The pain she saw flickering in the dark pupils of his eyes made her feel guilty for involving him. She had used Charles in a despicable way. She had destroyed his dreams along with her own. Would this encounter psychologically scar him? she wondered. The male ego was reputed to be fragile. She had to free him from any doubts about his own sexual prowess.

"Not true," she argued. "Don't you see? I used

you, knowing the odds were against the chance of my being able to respond."

"No, I don't see," he replied abruptly, his voice rising. "You were grasping at straws trying to keep afloat, but you didn't *use* me!"

Johanna could feel her chin beginning to wobble as new tears threatened to fall. He wasn't going to listen. The burden of what had happened was sitting squarely and visibly on his hunched shoulders.

"Did Bill do this to you?" he asked, slicing through the silence and the self-pity she was sinking into.

Harsh laughter and a single tear were wrenched from Johanna. A bubble of hysteria was close. "It's *me*, Charles . . . *me!*"

"No," he shouted, grasping her shoulders and administering a gentle shake before clasping her tightly against his chest. "You responded to a point, then withdrew. You're no more frigid than I am." Her fingers clutching the cotton of his shirt spoke volumes. He could feel the fabric tangling against his chest. "Love . . ." he whispered, "I promised our loving would be good. Good for both of us. Admittedly I didn't expect what happened, but it did. Now I know more about you and about your reasons for coming to me. You risked everything on one roll of the dice, one roll on the creek bank." His lips raked against her damp cheek. "We both deserve better odds than an all-or-nothing shot. Will you give me another chance?"

Johanna tensed. Go through it again? How could he expect her to risk such degrading humiliation *again?* She wasn't a masochist. It hurt too badly to have one's worst fears confirmed.

"Give me a chance, Johanna," he murmured near her ear. "Not here, not now, but soon."

Johanna plucked at the wrinkled shirt, weighing the risk against the possible reward. Had she unconsciously muddled her desire to have a child with the need to prove herself as a woman? No, her mind shrieked. She couldn't have deceived *herself,* could she? What about all the hours she had spent researching artificial insemination? Was that a cover-up for the real problem? She couldn't seem to figure herself out.

"Can I think about it?" she hedged, evading his eyes.

"My gut-level feeling is you've thought about it too much. You've come up with . . . clinical solutions for emotional problems. You're thinking with your head and discounting your heart." Setting her away, he moved closer to the creek's bank where his loafers were and slipped his bare feet into them, then mated the one dry sock around the wet one.

He's disappointed . . . angry, she silently moaned. *I've managed to hurt both of us.*

"Forgive me?" she asked, knowing he couldn't.

"Can I think about it?" he sarcastically mimicked, striding away from the creek bed.

For a moment, she was stunned by his reply. The patience and consideration he had displayed when comforting her was gone. She had hurt him again, deeply.

"No!" she shouted in answer to his question, running to catch up with his long strides.

Swinging around, hands on hips in a belligerent stance, Charles yelled, "Dammit, Johanna. You're asking too much! Oh, hell, what's the use? Take the easy way out. Go to the hospital and get yourself impregnated!"

Stopping in her tracks, she listened to his outburst of anger and frustration. "What's wrong? Can't keep your hands-off promise?" she baited. Her reasons for wanting a baby were still murkier than the muddy Mississippi, but she knew without a doubt that she loved the man stalking toward her with slow, determined steps. A broad boyish smile of delight replaced his scowl.

"You won't regret the choice you made," he said huskily, wrapping his arms around her shoulders. "Trust me, love. I've been wrong more times than I care to admit, but this time"

—he paused long enough to hug her swiftly, planting a kiss on her uptilted lips—"this time, I'm going to be right."

Johanna clung to Charles. They were both taking a chance. Taking a chance that could fulfill their every dream or make their lives a nightmare of failure.

CHAPTER SIX

Crossing the high rows of soybeans, they silently headed back to the farmhouse. Charles could feel Johanna's footsteps dragging with each step.

"I'm not going to bounce on your bones at the slightest opportunity," he teased, releasing her shoulder and lifting her hand to his mouth. "Don't tense every time we get near a room with a bed."

"Programmed response," she admitted softly. "Bill evaluated every dwelling by the size of the bedroom."

"Only the bedroom?" Charles asked, nibbling the fleshy part of her thumb. "In the dark?"

Johanna nodded. Regardless of how uncomfortable she felt talking about her previous experiences, she realized any insights she gave Charles could be the key to unlocking her problem.

"You'll have to tell me what you like and don't like, love. Do you want me to stay at the motel tonight?"

With a shrug, Johanna nonchalantly said, "You're the doctor. I'll trust you to make the right decisions."

"I'm not infallible. If I stay, I'll hold you . . . nothing more." He stroked his thumb over her wrist, testing for an accelerated pulse.

"I'd like that," she acquiesced, taking his hand and rubbing the soft hairs on the back of it against her cheek.

"Are you hungry? Emotional upheaval sets off my appetite."

Smiling, Johanna responded easily, "Starved. The cabinets are bare, though. I had planned on having a quick sandwich in town on the way out here."

"Care to rearrange your plans to include a nice leisurely dinner?" he offered, opening the trunk to get their suitcases.

"Such a silver-tongued salesman," she quipped glibly. "You missed your calling."

Chuckling, he firmly closed the lid, took her

hand, and led the way into the house. The aging wooden steps and porch creaked, as did the screen door when it was opened.

"Seems to be in good shape," Johanna commented as they stepped into the hallway. "I leased the land to Bubba Rhoades. Remember him?" she asked as they stripped off the dusty white sheets that covered the upholstered furniture and folded them.

"Sure I do. Why is he farming your land? His dad is the local land baron, isn't he?"

"I guess he's doing it as a family favor. The Rhoadeses and the Jenkinses have been friends for as long as I can remember. Being an absentee landlord can be tricky. You have to find someone you can trust, and who trusts you."

Johanna picked up the stack of dusty linens, walked through the kitchen, out to the screened-in back porch, and dumped them on a painted wooden table. The sight of acres and acres of land with row upon row of crops never failed to have a healing effect upon her. She remembered as a child sitting on this same porch late at night listening to her grandparents and the neighbors from nearby farms discussing rainfall, the cost of seed and new equipment. Since their deaths the silence had been broken only by the chirping of crickets, the imagined sound of plants growing, and occasionally Bubba and his wife and children dropping by for a visit.

I'll have to call Bubba and let him know I'm here, she thought. Johanna grinned. The last time she had arrived unexpectedly, Bubba had almost scared her to death by sneaking into the house, shotgun in hand, and giving an Arkansas Razorback battle cry as he barged into the bedroom.

"Pleasant memories?" Charles asked as he leaned against the frame of the kitchen door watching her profile.

"Yeah. I've had a lot of happiness here."

Johanna's eyes flickered from Charles's dark hair down to his loafers. She knew he was city-born and bred, but he seemed to belong. She watched his eyes sweep over the land as he inhaled deeply, his chest expanding to accommodate the fresh air, stretching his knit shirt tightly over his muscled chest.

"Do you know . . . I loved and hated this farm all at the same time?" he asked, his lips turned up at the corners.

"You loved coming here, or so you said. Why did you hate it?" she asked, perplexed.

Charles extended his arms, motioning with his fingertips for her to come closer. Johanna walked into them as though it was something she had done every day of her life for years and years.

"I hated your leaving St. Louis and coming down here for weeks on end to visit your grandparents."

Johanna chuckled as she looked up at him. "I spent many a night, lying in bed, wondering if you were out with some gorgeous blonde," she confessed.

"And I spent the same nights worrying about Bubba uniting the farms by seducing you," Charles growled.

"Bubba and I were friends, nothing more," Johanna argued.

"Hmmm. So you said at the time, but that didn't keep me from wondering."

"Well, you'll be glad to know Bubba married the banker's daughter and has a passel of kids," she said, smiling.

It was wonderful to be able to talk about things they had stuttered and stumbled over as teenagers. She had been constantly unsure of Chuck's feelings, and apparently he had been equally insecure about hers. How comforting to be able to confide in each other now. She had nothing to hide; he already knew the worst.

"Ready to go to dinner?" Charles asked, not wanting her to sink from her present buoyant mood.

"I'm ready."

Hand in hand they walked through the house and back out to the car. It wasn't long until they were seated in Sikeston's finest restaurant, orders placed, sipping a light, fruity white wine.

Charles thoughtfully swirled the wine in his stemmed glass. There were so many questions he needed to ask, but he couldn't find a subtle, unoffensive way of asking them. He tipped the glass against his lips and emptied it.

"You're supposed to be plying *me* with liquor," Johanna teased.

"My silver tongue is tarnishing in my mouth," he replied, laughing, as he laid his hand over hers on the white linen tablecloth. "I'm wrestling with a way to ask you some questions that aren't the usual topic for dinner conversation."

"Such as?"

"Artificial insemination. How much do you know about it?" he queried, topping off her half-filled glass before filling his own.

"Facts?" she asked, raising an eyebrow and watching him nod his head.

"Thousands of babies each year are born due to AID, Artificial Insemination by Donor. It's not painful and can be done in a physician's office."

"Doesn't your not being married eliminate you from the procedure?"

"Actually, from what I've discerned, there are few state or federal laws regarding AID. Most doctors require the patient and husband to sign a form agreeing to support any child derived from the procedure, but that's about it." Lifting her shoulder, she concluded, "You can even pick out what physical characteristics you prefer."

"Who are the donors?" Charles quizzed, unable to fathom any man being willing to deposit his seed in such a sterile container.

"Med students. Resident doctors. Volunteers." Johanna sipped her wine, watching for some reaction on his face. "A couple of years ago there was an article in one of the national magazines about Pulitzer prize winners being asked to make . . . donations." Discussing this topic in a matter-of-fact manner, as though they were talking about the weather, made her adopt the tones of a teacher explaining something to a child.

"Why does the book *1984* keep running around up here?" he asked, tapping his forehead. "What do the parents tell the child when he's a teenager? You look like Albert Einstein because . . ." Taking another gulp, he emptied the glass again.

"Most parents don't explain. Why should they? I wouldn't."

The waitress bringing their food kept Charles's "Why?" from being answered.

As she cut a piece of steak away from the bone, Johanna mentally prepared herself to give an intelligent reply but couldn't find one. "The steak is delicious," she commented, switching the topic. Dropping his fork on his plate, Charles nearly choked on a bite of potato at the thought that entered his mind. "Is it possible for a donor to impregnate several women?"

"Possible, I suppose," she replied candidly, wondering why the question had been strangled.

"Don't you see? There's a possibility of incest down the line? What happens if your child, unaware of his beginnings, falls in love with another person with the same father as a donor?"

Johanna chuckled. "That's science fiction, my dear, the stuff novelists use to make a good read, or moviemakers capitalize on. Those possibilities are extremely remote."

Charles nodded his head. "I guess I'm rejecting the idea, the premise that women can have children without men." Flashing a grin in her direction, he added, "Another good plot could center around a world devoid of all men except one, whose goal in life is to destroy the sperm bank and become official stud for the female population."

"Does the thought appeal to you?" she asked, grinning at the preposterous idea.

"Impregnating the world is a teenage fantasy most young men indulge in," he replied in an offhand manner.

"Meaning monogamy is an institution built and maintained by women?" she quipped, openly laughing.

"Not all women are interested in monogamy," he said, watching her smile vanish.

"Are we speaking generally or specifically?" she inquired, wondering why he shared her bleak expression.

"Specifically, as in my case. Suzy had the exact opposite problem you have. She thrived on sexual encounters—with many partners."

"That explains—"

"Everything. Why I never remarried. Why I fantasized about you and your virtue. Why I . . ." Clamping his hand to the back of his neck, he massaged the muscles threatening to cause a headache. "Life was using the bottom of the deck when it dealt our hands, wasn't it?"

Absorbed by what he had said, she halted her fork halfway to her mouth. What could she say to help him? Wisely, she realized there was nothing she could say to eradicate his pain.

A cynical smile lifted one corner of Charles's mouth. "The two women in my life are at opposite ends of the spectrum. Finish your dinner, Johanna, and don't worry about it. I've coped with that particular memory for years."

She poked the steak between her numb lips and chewed the meat thoughtfully, wondering if she could favorably compete with the ghost of Suzy. Only to herself would she admit she had fantasized about replacing Bill's aggressive pace with the slower lovemaking she would enjoy with Chuck.

"Do men think about other women during—" The question blurted out before she could cap her mouth with her hand. A bad case of no filter between brain and mouth, she thought.

Genuine laugh lines crinkled near Charles's eyes. "Yes. Do women?"

A flush heightened the coloring in her cheeks. "Pass the salt and pepper, please," she requested.

"It's in front of your plate," he chuckled. "You've eaten all your steak and potato . . . what do you intend to spice up?" he bantered.

Scanning the table, she searched for any appropriate morsel of food. A roll, already buttered, was the single item available. Sprinkling a light coat of salt, then pepper, on the bread, she raised the concoction to her mouth.

"Will you eat that mess rather than answer your own question?" he asked lightheartedly.

"Ever tried it? Have a bite," she said, offering it to him with pseudo-innocence.

He pushed her hand away, laughing and shaking his head. "You answered the question. Now let's leave."

Perversely she took a teeny bite. "Yuck," she muttered, wiping her mouth on her napkin, then draining her wineglass.

Charles tossed a wad of green bills on the table and tugged Johanna's hand, pulling her out of the curved booth. They were both happy, laughing, and feeling mellow about each other as they left the restaurant.

Not having any hidden fears or secrets between them was exhilarating to Johanna. The tightrope she had carefully trod for ages seemed to disappear from beneath her feet. The effect was a heady, lighter than air sensation that carried her all the way to the car.

When they were headed in the direction of the farm, she leaned her head against Charles's arm, reveling in the lack of tension between them. They were getting to know each other again. The thought of having him share her bed, holding her throughout the night, suddenly held special appeal. She could trust Charles not to force her into intimacies she wasn't prepared for. How often she had longed to have him sleeping next to her. Smiling to herself, she wondered if he snored or tossed and turned, or worse, kicked.

"What's so funny?" Charles asked when he heard her laughter.

"Nothing," she said, smiling wider. "I'm just happy."

"Today has been a roller coaster ride, love. There is certainly no danger of being bored when you're around . . . especially with your weird food cravings," he teased.

"Who is it that eats peanut butter and bananas on crackers?" she asked, dredging up a memory.

"And cold pizza early in the morning? With Coke as a chaser?"

Snuggling closer, she quipped, "When I'm pregnant, you're probably going to eat the ice cream and pickles."

Charles's hand patted her bare shoulder. "That's further down the road than the farmhouse. Don't count your chick before it's hatched." The lilting humor sagged.

Driving into the lane, Johanna sat up and asked provocatively in a sultry voice, "Want to neck on the front porch?"

Ignition and lights were flicked off, and he gathered her into his arms. "Won't the man occupying the swing be shocked?"

Johanna bolted upright, peering into the darkness.

"Must be Bubba," she whispered, a note of regret easily discernible. She opened her car door and gracefully climbed out of the car, waving merrily.

A tall, broad form with a military bearing stood on the top step. With one athletic bound he was off the porch, swinging Johanna off her feet in a wide swoop. Squealing at the force of the exuberant greeting, she locked her fingers around his neck and held on for dear life.

"Put me down, you clodhopper," she laughingly teased.

"City slicker . . . you're all bones," Bubba's voice boomed. "Let's get married and I'll fatten you up."

Charles leaned against the car, one fist balled in his pocket as he watched Johanna's legs brush against Bubba's trunk-sized thighs. "She's spoken for, Bubba," he softly said in a casual voice that belied the core of steel determination beneath. "I'm Charles Franklin, remember?"

"Why, Chuck . . . you old dog. Are you still sniffing around my Johanna?" His powerful, calloused hand extended toward Charles as he dropped Johanna to her feet.

A bone-shaking grip later and a sound cuff on his shoulder, Charles asked, "Where's your bride?"

"Home with the kids," Bubba replied with a proud guffaw.

Johanna stepped between the two men, crooked her hands inside each of their elbows, and asked, "How about a beer, gentlemen?"

As the threesome walked up the steps, Charles's hand possessively slipped to Johanna's waist, only to find a ham hock already there. Glancing irritably down at Johanna, he caught her wink and felt his bicep drawn closer to the side of her breast.

The screen door squeaked loudly as Charles opened it and Bubba opened the front door.

"Get us a beer, scrawny one, and I'll arm wrestle Charles for the pleasure of sitting next to you on the love seat." Bubba flexed his muscles.

"Quit teasing," Johanna reprimanded. "Beer at the kitchen table is the best I can do." One finger shaking at his midsection, she warned Bubba, "Crissy would alter the size of your ears with a rolling pin if she heard you."

"Aw shucks, ma'am," Bubba said in the dialect city folks expected of farm boys, "I won't do nuthin' which ain't circumspect." Twisting his foot in a small circular motion with pseudo-bashfulness, he beamed Johanna a country-boy smile.

Cuffing his shoulder, Johanna laughed at the

hick-farmer routine. "Knock it off, congress-man."

Charles's eyes widened as he drew a chair across the worn linoleum and waited for an explanation.

"Bubba is running for state representative," she said, unlatching the door on the ancient refrigerator and plucking out two beers and a Coke. "Crissy is diligently grooming him to walk as though he doesn't have a row of corn between his legs," she said impishly to Bubba as she passed him a beer.

Bubba tossed back his head, roaring with laughter. He tilted back his chair on two legs and said confidently, "I'm a shoo-in with my good looks and country-boy charm."

Groaning, Johanna collapsed into an adjacent chair. "The crops are looking good. Am I going to lose the best farmer a girl ever had if you win?"

"Naw! Politics and farming mix. With farm prices low, I'll need the winter income to make ends meet." Bubba twisted toward Charles, nearly overbalancing. "Your intentions are honorable, aren't they?" he asked, with a bright glint in his eye.

"Bubba!" Johanna protested, embarrassed by the unexpected blunt question.

"Just checking him out. Don't want to see my

landlady getting messed around," he jibed, assuming a fatherly pose as he lowered the front legs of his chair to the floor.

"Bubba Rhoades, I'm going to vote three times for your worthy opponent if you don't zipper your mouth," she threatened.

"I'm not married," Charles offered pointedly, softly, dangerously. "And I don't have a passel of kids, either."

Slapping his thigh, Bubba chuckled. "Guess that puts me in my place." Draining his beer, his Adam's apple bobbing, he set the empty bottle on the table. "You staying a spell or headin' back?" he asked Johanna as he rose to his feet and tugged his jeans back into place.

"Heading back in the morning," she replied, arching her head back to keep contact with his eyes.

Charles stood. "I'll see you out," he offered briskly.

"You leaving, too?" Bubba asked with a devilish smile. "It is getting late."

"City slickers keep late hours," Charles suavely replied with a roguish twist of his lips.

"Guess that explains my having six kids . . . early to bed, et cetera, et cetera, et cetera. By the way, Johanna, I limed the back forty. The bills will be in your semiannual statement." Bending, he kissed her cheek with brotherly affection. Gesturing toward Charles, he added cryptically, "Remember where you come from." Straightening, he extended his hand toward the man waiting at the kitchen door. "Nice seeing you again, Chuck. Don't bother seeing me out."

After he heard the front screen slam shut, Charles cocked his head toward the noise and asked, "What did he mean by his parting shot?"

"Remember where you come from?" Shrugging her slender shoulders, she narrowed the gap between them to mere inches.

Charles hooked his hands at the back of her waist; their bodies touched from hips to knees, and pursued the question. "Well?"

Laughing upward, Johanna shook her head and brushed seductively against his chest. "Bubba spent his teenage years trying to impregnate all the virgins in eastern Missouri. Now as a pillar of the community, he reminds everyone of their Puritan Bible Belt roots."

"The reformed rake?" he quizzed.

"Mmmm." Unable to stop herself, she yawned widely, covering her gaping mouth with one hand. "Crying exhausts me. Ready for bed?"

"Will I wake up looking into the wrong end of a double-gauge shotgun?"

"That's a chance you'll have to take," she said

lightly, pulling him with one finger stuck through his open top buttonhole.

"You go ahead. I'll lock up," he offered softly, giving her time to get ready for bed in privacy.

"No locks," she murmured sleepily, "except the padlock on the outside. Scared?"

"Witless, but not of the Jolly Green Giant," he replied with a rueful grin. "Sleeping with you is going to be the supreme test of self-restraint."

"Worried?"

"Who's reassuring whom?" he asked with a chuckle.

"Oh, I'm plenty brave until I cross the threshold of the bedroom."

"In that case," he said, deftly swooping her off her feet, "I'll eliminate the problem by carrying you."

Johanna reached behind him to switch off the light. "No et cetera, et cetera, et cetera?" she said, a tremor in her voice.

"None," he reassured her, cradling her head against his shoulder. Nudging the bedroom door open with one foot, he heard a nervous laugh from beneath his chin and knew she was beginning to tense up.

"It'll be okay."

Johanna willed herself, unsuccessfully, to relax. *This is Charles holding you like a treasured piece of fragile glass,* she told herself. Slowly, she felt herself being lowered to her feet.

"Get your nightgown and change in the bathroom," he murmured considerately. "Some night in the future I'll enjoy watching you slip out of your clothes"—he stroked the nape of her neck with sure fingers—"but we'll learn to walk before we run." Turning her toward the suitcases, he lightly shoved her in the right direction.

CHAPTER SEVEN

In the bathroom, Johanna completed her nightly ritual in record time. The sleepiness she had felt earlier was replaced with a bright anxiousness in her dark eyes. Face scrubbed clean, hair brushed to a gleaming sheen, she spritzed a light spray of perfume on each pulse point.

She could hear Charles preparing for bed in the adjoining room. When she heard the featherbed creak, she knew he was waiting. Johanna fought the urge to wring her hands. She trusted him, didn't she? *Hell, I trusted Bill, too*, she thought. Smoothing the satiny length of her nightgown along her thighs, a bubble of pain welled in her throat.

"Why are you doing this again?" she asked herself quietly as she rested her forehead on the cool mirror over the sink. If she had any sense, she'd get dressed and spend the night on the living room sofa. Johanna shivered as the overhead air conditioning vent blew cool air across her bare shoulders.

"He won't hurt you," she argued, without confidence in the statement. She jumped when she sensed movement on the other side of the door.

"Did you fall asleep in the tub?" Charles asked. The coiled bedsprings squawked loudly, then she heard his bare feet making the wooden floors squeak as he crossed to the closed door. Johanna stared speechlessly at the only lock in the house. One flick of the wrist and he would be locked out. Hand trembling, she reached, twisting the doorknob, not the lock.

"Second thoughts," she joked weakly, walking into the bedroom but staying as far away as humanly possible from the man she would be sharing a bed with.

In the darkness she could not see the smile of understanding deepening the dimples in his cheeks. "Forgot my toothbrush. Can I borrow yours?"

"Yes." The monosyllable slipped through

tightly controlled lips while she lowered herself on the bed and eased between the sheets.

"Don't go away," she heard from the doorway.

Drawing the bedcovers up to her chin, Johanna's teeth began to chatter as she rolled to the side of the bed away from the doorway. *Stop it,* she ordered, curling into a tight, protective ball. *Relax,* she instructed, futilely.

Listening for sounds from behind the closed door, she heard the shower being turned off. *Quick shower,* she thought, wishing he had soaked for a year or so. Water splashed into the sink, almost drowning out the noises he made brushing his teeth. She squeezed her lids tightly shut.

The bed sank as it bore Charles's weight. When he leaned over her, a blend of Ivory soap and aftershave assaulted her senses.

"Are you expecting someone?" he teased softly.

Johanna didn't know whether he was teasing about her waiting for him, or whether he heard something outside that she hadn't.

"Do you hear somebody?" she whispered, listening carefully for any strange noises.

"No," he whispered over her shoulder; close but not touching. "There is so much space be-

113

tween us, I thought you were saving room for someone else."

Johanna was caught between laughing and crying. Her nerves were strung tighter than wire around a bale of hay. When she felt his hand touch her shoulder, she couldn't control the flinching response.

His touch withdrew. The bed shifted again as he rolled on his side away from her. "Good night, Johanna."

"Charles? Are you going to sleep?" she asked, aghast at his giving up after such a halfhearted attempt to make her feel at ease.

"Not likely."

Looking over her shoulder, eyes adjusted to the darkness, she saw the tense bunching of the muscles stretching his T-shirt over his back. "What do you have on?" she asked, expecting to see him garbed in striped, male pajamas.

"Underclothes."

"No pj's?"

"Don't own any."

"Oh," she responded, realizing he must usually sleep in the nude.

"I expected you to be in a granny gown," he teased softly.

Rolling on her back, Johanna crossed her arms behind her head and stared into the darkness. "I

haven't exactly been the epitome of coopera-
tiveness, have I?"

"No."

"Chuck, I'm just so damned scared. What if I
freeze up like I did at the creek?" Vulnerable,
hardly able to express her fear, she covered her
forehead with the back of her hand.

"I gave you my word. Doesn't that mean anything?" Charles asked, turning on his side to
face her.

"My heart hears you, but my head—"

"Listen to your heart. I would never intentionally harm you. You know that or you would
never have come to me. Trust me, love."

Blindly she moved the hand covering her
eyes to caress his face.

"Yes. Touch me," he crooned, inviting her ex-
ploration. "You're safe, love. Safe."

The hushed quality of his deep voice soothed
her frayed nerves. The heat of his mildly abra-
sive skin warmed her cold hands. Keeping her
eyes closed, she softly stroked the planes of his
face. High cheekbones, large eyes whose lashes
fluttered beneath her touch, straight nose, thin
upper lip, a fuller, sensuous lower lip were un-
hurriedly skimmed with featherlike strokes. She
was touching but not being touched.

"Chuck, hold me . . . please." The request
was barely audible.

He drew her near, and he closed the space between them, but he purposely kept their hips inches away from each other.

Cradled lightly in his arms, feeling cherished, safe, Johanna asked, "Can I take off your undershirt?" Her hand plucked at the cotton cloth covering his chest.

"Not yet, love," he responded, denying her request. Disappointed, she raked her nails over his cloth-encased back while she nuzzled his neck.

His hands caressed elongated circles from shoulder to waist, over the satin texture of her gown. A sweet, tingling sensation followed their path. "You have the softest skin," he murmured, continuing the caress to include the curve of her hip. "Satin over silk."

"Feels good," she whispered. "Luscious." Every muscle in her back relaxed. To return the pleasurable feeling, she began kneading the muscles below the nape of his neck.

Charles strung a fine line of kisses down her cheek as he raised her up until both their heads rested on the same pillow. He scarcely touched her lips.

Intoxicated by the minty flavor of his breath, she wound her arms around his neck and ran her fingers through the thick hair at the crown of his head. She sighed peacefully as she cuddled closer to his chest. She could hear and feel his heartbeat singing a quiet, comforting song.

"Let me take your shirt off," she requested again, desperately wanting to feel his skin touching her own.

"And your top?" His eyes smoldered as they bore into hers.

With one hand she reached to her waist and unsnapped the two hooks that held her gown in place. She sat up, and the moon bathed her golden-tanned skin with silver. Shrugging her shoulders and shedding the gown, she watched as Charles's eyes reflected the silver. He smiled tenderly.

The bed shifted as he sat up and stripped off his shirt in one fluid motion. Intentionally he moved his hips farther away as he watched her ease back onto the pillow. Her dark hair fanned into a wide, dark halo on the pillow, accenting her lovely face. Charles strove to control his passion. He wanted to bury his face in the shadowed valley between her breasts. He wanted to bring the flattened nipples to turgid life between his tongue and the roof of his mouth. He didn't.

When her hands brushed over the mat of hair on his chest, he schooled his face to keep smiling, to hide the desire raging in his bloodstream. Behind the smile he bit his tongue, and the distracting pain made primitive lust momentarily recede.

Lying back down, he drew Johanna back into his arms. He felt her breasts pucker as they touched his chest. They seemed to call to him in a language all their own. Charles ignored the physical request to love and stroke them.

"Go to sleep," he murmured, keeping tight rein on his passion, fighting a losing battle to keep control.

Johanna snuggled closer, enjoying the non-threatening clasp of his arms, and kissed the betraying, pulsating beat on Charles's neck. She was at peace, comfortably wrapped in the arms of the man she had loved for years. The dread, the fear, belonged to another woman. While Charles cursed the fates, Johanna praised them until she fell into a deep slumber.

Charles learned one lesson during the sleepless night: Promises, easily given, were sheer hell to keep. As dawn cast its light through the windows, he crept out of bed and stood, relieved that the dark hours were over. Glancing across the room, he saw Johanna turn and reach out for him.

"Chuck?" she whispered groggily. The empty hand balled into a fist. "Dream . . . dream," she said as though struggling to stay within the safe bounds of sleep. Sinking lower into the featherbed, pulling the sheet over her face, she retreated back to her golden world.

The lush curve of her feminine body was enticing. Charles mentally blasted himself for lusting, craving, torridly desiring a woman who needed patience and understanding. Under the cover of darkness he had caressed her body, inch by inch, like an agile pickpocket. Each part of her was imprinted on his hand and mind.

He had justified the sneak thief tactics by rationalizing that he was helping her by touching her when her conscious mind was not in control. Rubbing his hands over his raspy morning whiskers, he pulled her scent deep into his lungs like an aphrodisiac. She had responded, hadn't she?

The peaks of her breasts had seemed ready to burst beneath his gentle fingers. When his tongue swirled cautiously, she had arched, asking for more of the exquisite torture. For what seemed like hours, he had caressed and cupped the soft mounds. She hadn't awakened and rejected his meandering hands.

Johanna, he was certain, wasn't frigid. Re-creating their lovemaking beside the creek in his mind, he realized his mistake. He had taken for granted their state of arousal was mutual. It wasn't.

If his theory proved correct, they would soon

be more intimately entwined than plant roots binding themselves into the soil. If he was wrong, the promise would be broken and she would resort to . . . another means to reach her goal. Debating over which tactic to follow, he watched as Johanna rolled to her back, one leg bent, the other sprawled apart from the first. For a second, fear blocked his breathing, and he sucked in a gulp of air to calm himself.

Charles returned to the bed, slid between the tangled sheets, hesitated, then curved his arm slowly around her waist.

"Chuck?" she mumbled, hands covering her sensitized breasts.

The warm glow that had enveloped her dreams made her feel as though every nerve ending had come alive. Having Chuck share her bed produced the most erotic, sexual dreams she had ever experienced. She had willed the dream to never end, but it had.

An unfamiliar ache at the juncture of her thighs brought a smile to her lips. Had it been a dream? Or had . . . ? She didn't care. She wanted the kaleidoscopic colors painted on the inside of her lids to return again.

His moist lips surrounded her breast as she cupped it in her hand. She opened her eyes to see Chuck watching her, his head resting between her breasts.

"Love me, Chuck. Make me a woman," she pleaded softly.

His blue eyes darkened with desire, then he raised his head. He moved over her and took her mouth in hungry possession. His palms teased the pointed tips of her breasts. His tongue filled her mouth as her breasts filled his hands. He probed and kneaded with maddening intensity until desire boiled in her veins. She squirmed under his hands, and the friction of his coarse male hair rubbing against her own smooth skin was slowly driving her crazy.

He ended the drugging, mind-expanding kiss and weaved a pattern of kisses over her neck and collarbone, which blanketed her in a delightfully woven spell. The same sensuous pattern had been part of her exotic dream. She knew now the answer to her question: He had touched her during the night; touched her and made her bloom beneath his loving touch.

"You made love to me during the night." She spoke in a voice filled with wonder.

Abruptly lifting his head, Charles searched her face for scorn and saw only awe. "Not completely, but enough to know—"

Her fingertips covered his mouth, stopping the flow of words. "I wasn't frightened in the dream. Was I?"

"No. You were warm," he replied, a flush

121

stealing over his cheeks. "I felt like a boy stealing candy," he admitted.

"You stole nothing I didn't want to give you."

Restlessly his hand swept over the rounded globes of flesh to the curve at her waist. "Your body feels good under my hand. Touch me," he encouraged gently.

She rolled to her side and stroked him from shoulder to waist to muscled buttock. "You're like a sleek piece of polished wood, except you're warm, alive."

They kissed and spoke silent words of love and passion as Johanna molded herself against him.

Charles struggled to keep their hips apart. He knew he had to keep control. Deliberately his hand slowed the pace as it skimmed over her outer thigh in hesitant circles.

The closer his fingers came to the center of her being, the deeper Johanna buried her fingers into his back and buttocks. His hips, however, didn't budge an inch closer. She draped her leg over his upper thigh and entreated, "Touch me . . . touch me."

The bonds of restraint were crumbling when he lightly stroked the moist, womanly crevices. The evidence of her readiness, her passion, her desire, broke the one thread of self-control

Charles had remaining, and he thrust himself against her.

Johanna circled him with her hand, and she felt powerful when he quivered beneath her touch. Turning on his back, drawing her over him, he enticed her passion to fever pitch by saying, "Kiss me . . . love me until we explode."

With a dawning sense of strength, power, and tenderness, Johanna guided their bodies together. She marveled at the fantastic sensations as she slowly sank, luxuriating in their being together as one.

Loving Chuck was a world apart from any other experience. She was the dominant force in the tempo, but being in control held new responsibilities. Quickly cued by his body language, she increased the pace when she felt his hips arch, and slowed when his hands languidly stroked her hips.

In a hushed voice Chuck painted a fantasy behind her lids. They were in the desert, riding across the sands together. His fingers trailed lightly over her torso as he spoke of the sun and the wind. She was on a fabulous journey; an ecstatic journey with the man she loved, the man who loved her.

Johanna licked her lips, almost tasting the sand as it blew around them. Tossing her head back, she welcomed the sun's heat. In her mind's eye she could see them riding faster and faster, faster than the wild wind.

"Chuck!" she cried. "Chuck!" A final burst of speed brought the colors of an oasis blindingly close. Chuck shuddered beneath her, sharing the joy.

She collapsed against the muscled hardness of Chuck's chest, breathing heavily. She could taste the salt of his perspiration.

"Easy, love. Easy, my love," he sang, his hand gentling her trembling body. "You're safe in the arms of your lover. Safe, shhhhhh, safe."

Johanna's smile of satisfaction was wide and full of happiness. "Chuck, I've never felt anything like that."

Their glorious lovemaking had freed her. She soared like a bird just released from its cage.

Chuck rolled her to her side and kissed the hollow of her throat. "Answer the question you avoided at dinner about what women fantasize when they make love. Did you see me?"

"Possibly," she teased, nestling her hands in the short hair at the back of his head. "I think we might want to field-test your theory to be certain."

"Imp!" he exclaimed, fingers tickling her ribs. Their combined laughter filled the room with joy.

"Chuck . . . thank you."

Taking her wrists and spreading them on either side of her head, Chuck leaned over her and said solemnly, "Don't thank me, love. The pleasure was mutual. I only wish . . ." *I had been the first. That you hadn't had to suffer with those doubts. That I knew it was my face you saw.*

"What? What do you wish?" she inquired huskily as the hairs on his chest lightly stoked the banked fires in her chest.

"That you'd answer my question." Thoughtfully, he paused, realizing his own insecurities were showing. "I need to know because—"

"Because you weren't my first lover?" she asked cautiously.

"Right," he admitted. "I was never the man Suzy saw. I 'scratched an itch'—her words, not mine—but was never the man she saw when we made love."

"Chuck, there are many reasons for making love. When we were teenagers, had we 'gone all the way,' it would have satisfied my curiosity and proved your manhood. In my marriage, I stoically suffered through my marital obligations. But what we have . . ."

He freed her wrists as he listened intently, allowing her to hold his tormented face between the palms of her hands. Her brown eyes were shining with love.

"Whatever happened in the past, whatever happens in the future . . . it's your face I'll see, and your name I'll be calling."

For several seconds, Chuck shut his eyes. The savage wounds he had suffered were beginning to heal for the first time. He could feel his heart twisting, righting itself in his chest. He felt renewed, like a new man.

"No fears?" he questioned.

Johanna searched the corners of her mind for any doubts, and found none. She did not fully understand what had taken place, but his eyes were weaving their magic spell again. Slowly, she answered the question with her lips. Everlasting love, she felt, couldn't be expressed with mere words.

CHAPTER EIGHT

"Why don't you let me drive?" Johanna asked as she slammed the trunk lid down after Charles had stowed their suitcases inside. A cheeky grin reflected her glowing mood. "You had a . . . long night."

"Be my guest." He handed her the keys and opened the driver's door.

Johanna started the car as he walked around the front of the car to the other side. The warm glow of their early-morning lovemaking was fresh in her mind. She appreciatively watched his lithe, athletic movements. *He may be tired,* she thought, foot pressing on the gas pedal, *but he is one well put-together man.*

"Racing your motor?" he teased, flashing her a heart-skipping grin. "Or planning on playing the Black Widow game?"

"Love 'em and kill 'em? It's the female version of the human male's love 'em and leave 'em," she bantered, winking audaciously.

"Neither applies to us," he commented as his hand slid over her knee and lingered on her bare upper thigh. "Nothing like short shorts, on long, slender legs," he complimented.

"I'm glad you didn't call them hot pants," she jested, flexing her leg muscles.

"Wishful thinking on the part of a lecherous advertising exec."

Minutes later they were headed back to St. Louis on the pancake-flat interstate highway. Their light conversation was punctuated by meaningful pauses and glances. Charles stretched his legs as far as the plush car interior allowed but was still cramped.

"Want to put your head on my shoulder?" she asked as he twisted, trying to get comfortable.

"Shoulder . . . lap . . . backseat," he kidded. "What I need is a featherbed with a warm and willing Johanna Jenkins curved around me." Finally crossing his legs and scrunching low in the seat, he relaxed. "If you want me to take over, wake me up," he quietly offered.

The swelling music from the quadrophonic

speakers caught her attention when a popular Lionel Richie song began playing. The lyrics matched her mood, and she hummed along with the chorus.

Generally she disliked the trip back to the city —it always seemed so long. Today she could have driven via Kansas City and it would not have mattered. *I'm happy,* she mused, relishing the feeling. *I'm genuinely, no-artificial-flavoring-added happy.*

The feeling of being at peace lasted throughout the trip home. As they neared the city, she gently shook Charles's arm. "My place or yours?" she asked, distracted from driving when he stretched over and caressed her leg.

One eye drowsily opened. "Your prerogative, Lady Johanna. I don't care whose castle we live in."

Johanna clutched the steering wheel. How could he bring up living together again? Was he bulldozing his way into her life? Was he taking her for granted already? A frown burrowed her forehead.

"Why don't we go to my place, then when you're ready to leave, your chariot will await you," she suggested with a wry note of humor.

From the corner of her eye, she watched for his reaction. Nothing. Not a blink of an eye, not a flexing jaw muscle, absolutely no overt response registered on his face.

"Is tomorrow a working day for you?" she questioned.

"Mm-hmm. No rest for the wicked," he replied, sitting up, glancing around to orient himself. "I have a sixteen-year-old patient coming in that I'm not anxious to see."

Johanna knew Charles was guiding the conversation away from the live-in-lust topic. Did he think she was now sex-starved enough to enter into a casual physical relationship? He'll have to *re*think, she decided, not listening to him.

". . . teenagers. They're singularly cruel to anyone wearing glasses. Poor kid isn't as lucky as you are. I've tried every lens the major manufacturing companies put out and she can't read the line below the big *E.*"

"Nobody's vision is *that* bad," she commented, keeping the conversation stringing along until she was in the safety of her own home.

"Some people can't read the handwriting on the wall when it's in bold, red script," he cryptically replied with a tight grin.

"On the other hand, there are those who read between the lines when there isn't anything there to be read," she retorted.

Johanna turned off the highway, driving into the setting sun. Lowering the sun visor, she grappled in her purse for her sunglasses.

Charles pushed her hand aside and opened the zipper compartment she had been fiddling with. Holding them up, he quipped, "I'm glad they aren't rose-colored." He placed them in her outstretched hand and added, "Your vision is distorted enough as it is."

"The Missouri Department of Vehicle Licensing disagrees with you, doctor. Last year I passed the test with flying colors."

"Things change from year to year . . . day to day in your case."

Johanna was relieved to see her condo complex immediately on the right. The double entendres were becoming too close to the obvious to be comfortable.

"It's been a wonderful trip," she said, which she hoped would lead to a polite thank-you-for-a-pleasant-day good-bye response. But was that what she wanted? A casual kiss at the door after their intimate weekend was ludicrous. What other choice did she have? She couldn't stand a relationship without commitment, a relationship based only on physical need. *Break it off neatly while you can,* the sane portion of her mind advised.

"Glad you enjoyed yourself. We'll have to do it again," he responded with courteous glibness.

Parking the car beside her own, Johanna dropped the keys in his lap, avoiding looking at the devilish smile she knew was plastered on his face. He had always been able to make mundane talk have a double meaning.

Johanna opened her door, stepped out, stretched her legs and arms, then walked to the rear end of the car. Why didn't I keep the keys? she groaned silently. *Now he'll get my suitcase out of the trunk and have a gentlemanly excuse for entering my home.* The chuckle she heard when he lifted her case out made her wonder if she'd spoken aloud.

Keeping her shoulders straight, consciously stopping her hips from swaying provocatively, she led the way to her doorstep. She pasted a wide, artificial smile on her face, unlocked the door, and turned to face him, saying, "Thanks again."

His blue eyes raking her from head to toe, Charles deposited the overnight bag inside the doorway and braced himself in the narrow opening.

"Anytime, love."

Silence, heavier than the humid air, hung between them. What could she say to a man who confused her every sane thought with a dose of passion? Offer him her hand? How bizarre! Kiss his cheek? She felt Charles touch her flushed cheek lightly.

"Think about it. We both need to reassess our thinking." With a fleeting caress of fingertips to her lips, he said, "Keep in touch." A whisper of a kiss later, he quickly swung around and retreated to his car.

Walking away from Johanna was the most difficult thing he had ever done. He prayed he could cover the short distance without having his shaky legs collapse beneath him. He knew his gait was awkward, jerky. Fumbling in his pocket for his keys, he glanced over the roof of the car and saw Johanna mutely standing in the doorway.

Don't crawl back, he told himself. *Wave nonchalantly and get in the car.* After accomplishing both feats, he struggled to keep from resting his head on the steering wheel in fatigue. *She doesn't want you, man. Get the hell out of here before you make a complete bumbling ass out of yourself.*

Backing out of the driveway, he concentrated on the mechanics of driving a car as though he had never sat behind the wheel. He shifted the automatic transmission into drive; his right foot slipped from the brake onto the gas pedal. The result was a short stretch of black rubber left on the road as he roared out of the parking lot.

"Teenage stunt," he muttered, embarrassed by the meaning Johanna would find in his abrupt departure.

"Couldn't get out of here fast enough, could he?" Johanna mumbled, entering the cool interior of her condo. "What did you expect?" she asked, continuing the one-sided conversation. "You chased him, challenged his male virility with frigidity, practically raped him, then absurdly rejected him as though you were a teenage virgin. What a screw up!" she flung into the silent room.

She picked up a decorator's pillow from the couch, punched it once, then drew it to her chest to comfort the pain she was feeling in the region of her heart. *Romantic fool,* she chastised, flopping down on the sofa, still hugging the pillow close.

Shivering, she realized the room was cold. *Who cares?*

"Nobody," she muttered, indulging in a moment of self-pity. Raising her head to watch the setting sun filtering through the long, floor-to-ceiling windows, she physically shook off the depression that threatened to swamp her.

"Get busy," she ordered her body.

Her gaze circled the room, searching for

134

something to clean or straighten. The place was immaculate. She plumped the pillow and neatly placed it on the couch as she eyed the suitcase by the door. Unpacking and doing the wash held little appeal, but it was better than crying her eyes out on the sofa. With a determined grunt, she picked up the green bag and traipsed into the bedroom.

The sight of the double bed made her fingers stiffen, clutch. She didn't think she would ever be able to look at a bed without seeing Charles sprawled on it, laughing, teasing . . . loving.

"Knock it off!"

Exasperated with herself for the weakness she couldn't get rid of, she flung the suitcase on the bed with more force than necessary.

"Back to Plan *B*, you fool. Don't let what happened blow you off course away from your goal."

Sorting through her hastily packed bag, she smiled. A baby was something she could look forward to. *A baby with dark hair, turquoise-blue eyes, and long fingers clasping my fingertips.* Shocked at the small image of Charles she had created, she altered the picture to a curly-haired, blond-headed, brown-eyed infant. It didn't work: The hair and eye color changed back despite her efforts.

Giving up on erasing the image, she walked to

the closet and got out her sketch pad, ink, and watercolors. She piled the artist's materials on her lap as she reclined in the armchair beside the bed. She reverted back to the method she had used since childhood to relieve tension. Had it been her father who told her, "Paint your dreams"?

Strong, bold lines later, a profile lay beneath her pen point. She groaned aloud as she traced her fingers over the drying lines, smudging the image of Charles. Resolutely she drew a huge X over the page and flipped it to the next blank page.

As she began drawing a cherubic, round baby face, she decided to wait on the watercolors. The color could be added later—much later— when she had recovered her sanity.

"Self-serving, lying, hypocritical . . . *toad!*" Johanna shouted at the man who had seconds ago hung up his end of the phone. "Call me at the end of the week with a decision!" she quoted.

Fuming, Johanna was tempted to wreak havoc on everything in sight. The porcelain figurine would smash delightfully against the wall, she thought. Shredding the foam stuffing from the pillows on the sofa would be better. Johanna clenched and unclenched her hands as she fought to gain control of her temper.

She could picture the scrawny-necked, shriveled principal leaning back in his desk chair gloating. He had fought her tooth and nail for twelve years over the district's outdated curriculum, and now . . . now that she had resigned, he had been "authorized by the school board to contact her in regard to a new coordinator's position that had become available."

That piece of Milquetoast presented my *ideas and took the credit,* she mentally spat. *I have a good mind to contact the superintendent and take the blasted job!*

Johanna stomped barefoot into the kitchen, away from the possessions she was threatening to destroy. She reached into the refrigerator and grabbed the carton of milk. After she filled the glass, she chugalugged the contents. The phone jangled again just as she slammed the empty glass on the counter top.

When she had received the first call she had been too stunned to react, but now she knew exactly what she'd say to that crowing rooster. With each step she muttered a foul expletive.

"Hello," she growled, ready to tell him exactly what she thought of his backstreet, knife-in-the-back tactics.

"Did I catch you at a bad time?" Johanna

heard through the receiver. The voice was deeper, huskier than the one she had expected to hear.

"Who is this?" she demanded in a strident, it-had-better-not-be-a-solicitor voice.

"Charles. Don't you recognize my voice?"

Johanna adjusted the phone between her ear and shoulder. Two weeks had passed since she had heard his voice. Now, when she least expected it, he was calling. Had he been waiting until she was sufficiently love-starved?

"Long time no see," she quipped coolly, coating the words with a liberal sprinkling of sarcasm as she threaded her fingers nervously through her hair.

"Didn't you get my gift?"

"What gift?" she sputtered, confused.

"The tomato plant," he explained slowly.

Johanna's eyes widened in surprise. "I thought Bubba sent it to remind me of my roots," she gasped, revealing more than she would have had she not been taken off guard.

"Do you usually receive gifts from your farmer friend?" Charles asked in a strangled voice.

"That's a leading question," Johanna responded, chuckling and twisting the coiled phone cord between her fingers. "Didn't you

know my doorstep is perpetually *filled* with tomato plants?"

Charles's laugh was breathy, anxious. "I considered minks, diamonds, and fur coats, but rejected them as unromantic."

"Tomato plants may not be listed under the
heading 'trite gifts,' but . . . romantic?" she
asked, her voice lilting.

"The poem was romantic, wasn't it?"

"What poem?"

"The one tied on with a passionate pink ribbon."

"A tomato plant with a frilly ribbon attached
was all I found on my doorstep. No note . . .
poem or otherwise."

"That's why you didn't call," he responded,
relief evident in his voice. "You've put me
through hell the past two weeks, woman."

The thought of him suffering as she had, momentarily delighted Johanna. Were his finger-
prints smudged on his phone because he constantly walked around with it in his hand to
prevent missing her call? Had he awakened in
the middle of the night and reached out, only to
find the bed had grown to king-size propor-
tions?

"I'm a mere shadow of my former self," he
complained lightly. "Down to skin and bones."

"Probably lost weight chasing your receptionist around the office," she tweaked.

"Mrs. Atkinson? You'll have to tell her that. She'll be flattered beyond belief."

Remembering Mrs. Atkinson's age, Johanna giggled into the mouthpiece.

"How are you, Johanna?" Charles asked after a short silence.

"Fine," she responded automatically. *Wretched,* she mentally amended.

"Not pining away?" he asked somewhat wistfully.

Yes! "No, I'm fine. Coping as usual."

A long pause stretched between them.

"I sincerely hope you're lying through your teeth," Charles said huskily. "Could I interest you in two tickets to anything showing in town?"

"Now that's the best offer I've had in weeks," she replied, not totally forgiving him for not calling sooner.

"I'd be insulted had you read my poem," he commented dryly.

"I'm tempted to search the bushes," Johanna replied, her curiosity piqued.

"Pick the time and place, and I'll recite it from memory," he joked halfheartedly.

"You're tempting me. How about Busch Stadium? The Arch? From the top of the flagpole on City Hall?" After each outrageous suggestion, she heard an increasingly loud laugh on the other end of the line.

"Make it easy on yourself," he cautioned.

"Hmmmm. Hadn't thought of damaging my own reputation. Of course, I can always pretend I don't know you."

"I suspect you've been doing a lot of that lately," he gibed. "But you're forgiven," he added in haste, remembering her anger when she first answered the phone. Skipping back to a safe subject, he asked, "How about the tickets? There are several good movies showing."

A kink in the coiled telephone cord kept Johanna's busy fingers from wrapping it past her knuckles. *I do want to see him,* she admitted, shaking her head over breaking the vows she had been making for the past two weeks. *I won't spend my time daydreaming over what could have been if I see him,* she promised herself.

"You'll always wonder about the contents of the poem if you refuse," Charles negotiated, tempting her curiosity.

"You could mail me a copy," she perversely suggested, stalling for time to make a wise decision.

"Could but won't."

"Charles, I don't think—"

"Good," he interrupted, "bad habit to get into

. . . thinking. Why don't I pick you up around six-thirty Friday night, and you can decide what you want to see then." He paused for a moment, then signed off, saying only, "See you."

Click. The phone transmitted nothing until the dial tone began to buzz.

"Oh, no, you don't, Charles Franklin," she whispered, dialing the number she had memorized weeks ago. The phone rang once. "You're not going to bully me. Johanna Jenkins makes her own decisions!"

"Glad to hear it, dear," Mrs. Atkinson responded. "Would you like for me to deliver your message dipped in arsenic or with an H-bomb attached?"

Johanna audibly groaned, her hand pressed against her forehead, her elbow braced against the wall. Quickly, she improvised, "Your boss is extremely pushy about selling contact lenses."

"And here I raised him to be such a mild-mannered man." Betty chuckled. "If he's only pushing you into contacts I'm sincerely apologetic. My motherly advice must not be working."

Though her mind worked furiously, Johanna couldn't come up with a witty response.

"You're making my job miserable, Johanna," Betty confided. "The boss alternates between an icy coolness and a raging inferno. I'm the one who suggested he bite the bullet, shove his pride to an unnamed place, call you, and not take no for an answer."

"Matchmaking, Mrs. Atkinson?" Johanna asked as she grinned at the older woman's confession.

"Just trying to hang on to my job so I can collect a healthy retirement check."

"Well, I wouldn't want to be responsible for you sweltering away in those long unemployment lines. Tell your boss I graciously accept his gallant offer to escort me to the theater," Johanna said primly.

"That news should keep the rent collectors from my door. Oh, uh . . . Johanna? Just to make certain I have food on the table for the next couple of years, would you mind splashing on an extra spritz of Estee?"

"You're incorrigible, Mrs. Atkinson," Johanna chastised.

"You're right. Everyone tells me so," she replied with pride. "Don't do anything I wouldn't do. 'Bye!"

Doused in perfume, Mrs. Atkinson would probably chase Charles around the desk, Johanna mused, smiling to herself.

A new, fresh bounce to her step, Johanna returned to the kitchen. She couldn't help grimacing at the droopy, bedraggled plant Charles had sent. The pink bow was surviving, but the brown tinges on the outer edges of the leaves and the yellowing at the base of the stalk predicted imminent doom for the plant.

Hadn't she done everything the horticulture book recommended? Watered it? Fed it? Placed it in a sunny window? *How dare it croak!* She snorted indignantly. Pouring one more cup of water on the dark, already wet soil, she attempted to save it.

CHAPTER NINE

By six o'clock Friday evening, Johanna was a basket case. Clothes were strewn from one end of her bedroom to the other in her quest to find just the right outfit. Standing in front of the mirror, palms perspiring, she sprayed perfume from head to foot.

"I need an antiperspirant for my hands," she muttered to the reflection staring back at her.

The entire day had been spent battling conflicting choices. Should she accept the prestigious job she had been offered or hold true to her motherhood goal? Had she been foolish to abruptly end the career she had loved for a chance at the unknown? And if she rejected the job offer in favor of motherhood, should she enter into an unwanted life-style with Charles or follow Plan *B?*

One hand smoothed the upsweep of dark hair to the top of her head as she reviewed the different paths she could take. The royal blue, vee-necked, full-skirted summer dress she wore was the result of the only decision she had made with any confidence.

"He's here," she breathed when the door bell rang.

Her poise was a facade as she greeted the man she loved with a sophisticated air kiss by the side of his cheek.

"You're beautifully bedecked," Charles complimented in a stilted, well-rehearsed voice.

He's as nervous as I am, Johanna realized, grinning at him as she took his hand and led him into the living area. "Thank you, kind sir. You look mighty handsome yourself."

"Lord deliver me from canned social speeches," Charles said, raising his eyes to the ceiling.

" 'Bedecked' makes me sound like a tinsel-covered Christmas tree," she teased, flicking an imaginary piece of lint from his light tan suit jacket.

" 'Kind sir' makes me sound like a senior citizen with one foot in the grave and the other on a banana peel," he replied as he captured her fluttering hand and rubbed it against his cheek.

"Shall we try again or give up on it as a lost cause?"

"Why don't we greet each other like long lost lovers?" Charles suggested, blue eyes devilishly twinkling.

"Because I spent three hours selecting what to wear, and I'd like to remain clothed for more than five minutes," she answered with provocative honesty.

"I do tend to rush my fences with you, but I'll try to control my animalistic urges." Instead, he sat down in the armchair and pulled Johanna along with him. "A stray cat would get better treatment at your doorstep than a kiss aimed for somewhere in space."

Leaning forward, Johanna gave him a swift, hard kiss before he could even close his eyes. She quickly scrambled to get off his lap but was instantly thwarted by one hand clamping on her neck, the other across her knees. Charles was chuckling as he nuzzled her arched neck.

"Keep squirming and I'll give you a big, purple, passionate hickey on your neck," he threatened, moistly sucking at the sensitive spot below her ear.

Her hands pressed against his chest, and she pushed with ineffective strength to no avail.

"Don't, Charles," she squealed. "What will people think!"

"They'll think you're extremely fortunate to have a man who makes passionate love to you," he countered, mumbling the words against her throat. His hand slid beneath her frock, sensuously touching the silky sheer nylons. "What's the verdict? Do you want a vampire kiss?"

Johanna cupped his chin and lifted his head then, curving her arms around his neck, she kissed him with all the pent-up passion she had vehemently denied them both. The male groan she heard encouraged her to part her lips, welcoming his probing tongue. The swirling, darting duel reminded her of the kisses they had shared in another time, another place. Twisting her head for closer contact, she pressed her aching breasts against his chest.

She felt his strong hands circle the soft flesh of her upper arms, easing her away, ending the kiss. His erratic breathing and the momentary flash of pain she saw in his eyes before they closed appeased her disappointment.

"Where do you want to go?" he asked, eyes remaining closed, no inflection in his voice.

Into the bedroom, she nearly blurted. Johanna slid off his lap to give them both breathing room and answered, "Anywhere."

"Nowhere?"

She searched his face for a concealed meaning. Was he referring to the plans for the evening or where their relationship was headed? She couldn't discern the intent behind his single word, nor could she explain her own reply.

Jackknifing to his feet, Charles crossed the room and stood, one hand kneading his neck, staring blindly out the front window. *I'm about to grovel,* he thought, disgusted with his lack of control. *I want her, damn it . . . on any terms.*

"We have to talk, Johanna, but not here." Glancing toward the hallway leading to the bedroom, he muttered to himself, "Unless . . . no, that would only complicate things further."

Johanna bobbed her head up and down in agreement as she moved to the front door. "Shall we?"

"We'd better," Charles replied with a half-grin.

Minutes later, after a silent car ride, they decided to have drinks and dinner at a nearby restaurant. Johanna twirled a glass of wine in her hand and tried to think of a safe topic to discuss to relieve the tension.

"I had an interesting interview today. My ex-boss offered me a new job."

"Doing what? Leading more teachers down your corrupt strike path?" he teased.

Ignoring the light gibe, she answered, "Writing a grant proposal for the state department."

"Sounds challenging. Going to take it?"

"They gave me a week to decide," she said thoughtfully. "It would mean tying myself to this area, which complicates my other plans."

His large hand covered hers as he asked, "Are pregnant ladies allowed to work for the district?"

Laughing at his outdated concept of teachers, she quipped, "The federal government isn't opposed to motherhood; the district doesn't have a choice."

"Then, where's the problem? Obviously the job intrigues you or you would have bluntly told them you weren't interested."

"The problem is"—she dabbed the moistness from her lips—"the legal stature of being an artificially inseminated mother."

"Who's to know? They don't stamp AID on your forehead, do they?" he asked with a weak grin.

"Of course not," she replied with a blandness she wasn't feeling. "But my continuously growing stomach might raise a few administrative eyebrows."

"Are you working up to a proposal?" Eyes bright, he picked up her hand and raked his lips over her knuckles.

Johanna was taken aback by his eagerness. Did he want her to propose? *No,* she thought, dismissing the possibility. He had made his attitude on that issue blatantly clear. Love together? Yes. Marriage? No.

"How about a sleepover party next Thursday night?" she asked, testing the water cautiously before plunging in.

He felt as though she had kicked him in the stomach with the impact of a Missouri mule.

Narrowing his eyes, Charles lightly placed her hand on the white linen tablecloth. "Back to your original plan of being impregnated by your first love?" he asked in a scathing voice. "Your expanding belly won't be a problem if I'm involved?"

"The district didn't fire an unmarried mother last year. I assume they would hesitate before making an issue out of . . . a *normal* pregnancy. Their viewpoint, not mine," she concluded.

"What happens if I refuse?" Charles asked bluntly.

"Plan *C,* I guess," she said, shoulders slumping forward.

"Another harebrained option?" he scoffed, avoiding her eyes by staring at the top of the high-backed chair she sat in. Pressuring her in the direction of marriage had failed. Grinding his back molars, he fought the urge to shake some sense into her head.

"Don't belittle a plan I haven't conceived yet," she tossed out in a clipped voice.

"My plan, A plus B equaling C, isn't acceptable?" he quizzed.

Johanna bit her tongue to keep from telling him how much she wanted him to father her child, but she wanted him to be a permanent part of her life. Loving him the way she did, living together would be disastrous. He'd feel responsible for the child, for herself, and feel obligated to legalize their situation. No way. She had married once for the wrong reasons, and one divorce in a lifetime was her quota, thank you very much.

"Your equation appears to be a sensible solution, but we both know it wouldn't work." Gently putting her hand over his, she added, "You've changed my life. I do hope we'll remain friends."

"Platonic friends make great lovers," he argued, not willing to be dismissed so casually.

"Great idea for an article for a magazine, but not for me," she replied, hoping the pain she felt wasn't detectable. "I'm the girl who prefers glasses to contacts. Remember?" she asked in a hushed tone.

The arrival of the waitress, pad in hand, kept Johanna from picking up her purse and leaving.

Their weekend together had not changed either of their viewpoints. The difference between living together and loving together was still the *I* Charles had referred to. Two weeks of not seeing or hearing from him had been miserable. What would living together, then watching him pack his belongings and walk out do to her? *No,* she thought, better for the two of them to continue to lead their separate lives.

"Steak okay?" Charles inquired coldly.

"Fine," she agreed, knowing the smallest bite would get blocked by the knot in her stomach. She watched Charles place the order, realizing this would be their last time together. He was angry. Perhaps that was best for him. Walking away would be easier if he sustained his present mood.

When the waitress left, an awkward silence developed between them. Both spoke simultaneously.

"Charles—"

"Johanna—"

"Go ahead," she offered politely, not knowing what she would have said to begin with.

"Johanna, would you consider . . . a mutually beneficial agreement between two old friends?" he asked, taking the last chance of keeping her. "If I agreed to"—the words caught in his chest—"impregnate you, would you live with me until you're sure you're pregnant?"

"You'd agree to fathering but not being a father?" she questioned, wondering what the next stipulation would be.

Hell, no! he wanted to respond but didn't.

"Yes," he capitulated.

"No stipulations?" she queried, forehead wrinkling.

"None that I will make. I always did think we'd make beautiful babies."

"What made you change your mind?" she asked cautiously. The devilish gleam in his blue eyes was hiding something.

"Maybe you'll decide you can't live without me," he said, nudging his knee between hers. "It's a pact," he continued, sliding his hand beneath the tablecloth, beneath her full skirt.

"Charles, behave," she gasped, grabbing at his marauding hands.

"Never," he whispered. "You'd be disappointed if I did." He grinned broadly, squeezing her silk-covered thigh.

Again, temporarily, she was his . . . until that fateful twenty-eighth day of her cycle. Then they would renegotiate their bargain. He'd convince her that Plan *C* should be legally marrying him. Marriage with all the children he could provide her with. The phrase "barefoot and pregnant" raced through his head. *Barefoot, pregnant, and mine,* he amended, then shifted the words around to *mine, then barefoot and pregnant.*

The euphoria Johanna had felt when they had driven back from the Bootheel was nothing compared to the champagne bubbling in her veins now. For once in her life she would have the whole apple: Chuck, her job, and a baby.

Dinner was eaten with zest. Anticipation was etched on both their faces.

"By the way, where's the poem you promised?" Johanna asked as coffee was served.

Charles flushed. "I was hoping you would forget. I'm not the most original person in the world when it comes to stringing words together."

"You said I could name the time and place," she reminded him. "Here and now will do nicely."

Napkin in hand, Charles wiped his mouth, then reached into his breast pocket. "One question: Did the plant survive?"

"The ribbon grew three feet," she teased, delaying the inevitable.

"The plant succumbed to a terminal case of Johanna Jenkins?" he concluded, shaking his head in mock disgust. Thrusting a folded sheet of paper toward her, he laughed. "My poetry can't be any worse than your plant-growing attempts."

Johanna unfolded the piece of paper slowly. A small green pellet dropped on the tablecloth. She read the note aloud:

"The tomato plant is not like me . . .
Can't survive on TLC.
Want to see the plant full grown?
Just pick up the telephone."

Giggling, she fingered the plant-food pellet on the tablecloth. "Why didn't *you* call?"

"Male pride," he answered succinctly.

"Women have pride, too," she pointed out as she refolded the note and put it in her purse. "You're the one who sped out of the parking lot as though the hounds of hell were in hot pursuit."

"Is that what you thought?" he asked.

"You gunned the motor," she accused lightly. "Don't tell me your foot slipped."

"It did."

"Sure it did," she laughingly scoffed. "Pull the other leg."

Charles leaned back in his chair. A smug smile he couldn't hide lit his face. He finally understood why she hadn't called. She'd misconstrued his clumsy departure. "I recall saying we needed to reassess our situation and to keep in touch. Would you have called?" he asked bluntly, all pretenses set aside.

"I could have come by to order contacts," she said.

"The day you wear lenses I'll know you've unconditionally surrendered to my charms," he said, laughing as he twined their fingers together.

"Don't you like women who wear glasses?" she joked.

Wickedly grinning, he leaned and whispered in her ear, "I won't object . . . if it's all you're wearing." Tugging on the golden hoop dangling from her ear, he said, "Let's go home."

"To feed the dying plant?" she asked.

"Among other things."

Unlocking the door to her condo, Charles blocked her entrance. "You want to carry me over the threshold?" he teased, watching the nervous expression on her face change to a smile. "I want you to be my equal. I carried you last time."

"How about side by side?" she suggested, laughing at the outrageous possibility of her being able to lift his bulk, much less being able to carry it anywhere.

His arm draped over her shoulder, hers wrapped around his waist as they went through the door with Charles intentionally pressing his hip against her to make it a tight squeeze.

"Whew! One of us ate too much dinner," he jokingly complained, closing the door with one foot. "We need some exercise to keep from getting fat and lazy," he suggested, pulling her against him.

Following the striped pattern on his tie with her fingertips, Johanna cocked one finely arched eyebrow and whispered, "What did you have in mind?"

"A swim in the pool?"

"You don't have a suit," she retorted as she tugged at the knot below his chin.

"Mmmmm. We'll have to think of something that I don't need clothes for," he suggested softly, nuzzling the nape of her neck. "Get your rubber ducky and we'll play in the bathtub."

Her fingers searched beneath his tie and unbuttoned the round buttons over his chest. "Sounds like good clean fun, but I'm a shower person."

"Better and better." His voice was husky, soft as finely spun velvet. His hands cupped the luscious curve of her bottom as he swayed against her. Kissing the corner of her mouth, he turned them both toward the bedroom. Instinctively he found and lowered the zipper at the back of her dress.

Piece by piece, they slowly undressed each other, spreading kisses over the bare, uncovered skin. Scanty bikini panties, the last garment for Charles to remove, were shed as Charles knelt, pulling them over her slender legs and watching her nimbly step out of them.

His hands stroking her bare hips, he kissed the thin red mark the elasticized band had made low on her hips. Arching against him, Johanna felt her knees buckling. Neither of them was teasing anymore.

Her eyes closed, she could only feel. The texture of his hair, the smooth satin skin covering his shoulders, the exquisite tapered fingers holding her partially upright as his lips nibbled from knee to inner thigh, were her undoing.

She heard her name spoken softly, reverently, as he lowered her until he could flick the tips of her breasts with his tongue.

"Charles . . . love," she crooned.

The pleasure-pain sweeping from her breasts to her womanhood made her hands clasp tightly around his shoulders. Johanna shuddered, passion and desire making her rock slightly back and forth in a sensuously teasing, tormenting rhythm.

"You feel so good," she whispered hoarsely,

biting the lobe of his ear as she sank down before him.

Charles lay her tenderly on the plush thickness of the carpet. "Not yet," he ordered, drawing his hips away.

"Yes, Charles. Love me. I want you," she begged, holding him, guiding him, wrapping her legs around his hips. She united their bodies, and that made her whole.

"This is where I belong," he uttered before fusing their mouths together in a burning kiss. Matching the movements of his tongue with those of his hips, he led her on another tumultuous journey; not with words, as he had done on their trip through the desert wasteland, but with the sweetness of unspoken tenderness and love.

Each silent stroke into her feminine softness was a tribute. Each reluctant withdrawal whispered volumes. Each motion took them beyond murmurs, beyond the barriers of language, to the mute words souls speak. The reincarnation of all their lives, all their souls, melted together in love's final thrust.

"My lover . . . my woman," he said hoarsely between tender kisses that branded her soft lips.

"Yes," she moaned during the brief pauses, reassuring, reaffirming the love bursting from her heart. "Yes, yes, yes."

They had shared desire, passion, physical fulfillment, Johanna realized as Charles collapsed beside her. Could they share the rapture, the ecstasy, for eternity? As if in answer, one shimmering tear, unnoticed by Charles, slipped from the corner of her eye.

CHAPTER TEN

The stinging sharpness of the shower's spray the following morning brought Johanna back to earth. Charles had loved her throughout the night. A sleepy caress was enough to ignite their passion. Neither of them could sleep for long as the need to physically renew the bond between them was ever present.

Johanna yawned. Warm water sprayed into her mouth and she drank thirstily. Her body tingled from his touch. There wasn't a millimeter of skin he had not touched with his lips or hands. She hummed a string of mellow notes; a silly grin spread across her face as she lathered from neck to toes, then languorously rinsed the suds off.

Had their compatibility during the night influenced the decision she had made during the small hours of the morning? Her back to the nozzle, she shook her head, letting the water stream through her hair. A new clarity of thought had come to her with the early-morning sun. Wanting a baby was secondary to her wanting . . . needing Charles. She realized her desire for a child had been the springboard leading her to Charles, but in reality she had been seeking what she thought was impossible.

She squirted shampoo into her hand, then spread it over her wet hair. She still wanted the child, she admitted, but she also wanted the father. She wanted a family. Holding her niece had initiated the dream; holding Charles throughout the night was what had made her whole.

Mentally she formed a new plan that included a romantic setting for the coming Thursday night—candlelight, champagne beside the bed in a silver bucket, soft music from the stereo, flowers throughout the house.

Humming louder, she sloshed water over the lathered hair she had piled high on her head. A glob of suds splashed down her spine, reviving the memory of Charles's hands lightly caressing the same path.

Her hair squeaky clean, she showered off and gracefully stepped out onto the carpeted bathroom floor. Wrapping a large bathtowel around her body sarong fashion, she finished by winding her hair in a turban. The mirror was thickly steamed, inviting an impulse to scrawl a message. With her index finger she drew a large heart with their initials in the center. Admiring her handiwork, she contemplated leaving the drawing to reappear when Charles took his shower.

"No," she murmured, admonishing herself for the teenage whim. A quick swipe with a hand towel removed the heart and the remaining moisture.

After hurriedly putting on a two-piece bathing suit, she finalized her plans for the day. Sketch pad in hand, she walked to the patio door and flung it open. The sun was shining, promising to make the afternoon blistering hot, but for now there was an early-morning coolness in the air.

Johanna relaxed into the multicolored floral cushion of the white wrought-iron patio sofa. The first page she turned to brought a grimace to her lips. *Why did I do that?* she asked herself, unable to understand her destructive X.

"Good likeness, too," she lamented, flipping to the picture of the child. A chuckle replaced her frown. She filled in the background with swirls of leaves intertwined with flowers, and mentally blocked in the dark wisps of hair and eyes the color of a semiprecious blue stone.

She used her finger to smudge and shadow the drawing until it gave the illusion of being three-dimensional. Sighing deeply, she admired her work. *Someday,* she promised herself, *I'll have a baby to love as beautiful as this one.*

She rested the pad on her bent knees and snuggled deeper into the pillows. Poor Charles, she commiserated, had to go in for Saturday morning appointments. She shut her eyes and memories of being held and loved led her to sweet, sweet dreams.

"I'm home," Charles shouted as he walked into the living room, shedding his perspiration-soaked jacket. "I'm home," he called again when Johanna didn't appear.

Sticking his head in each room, he felt a growing disappointment. He had expected a warm welcome, not absolute silence. He grinned, admitting to himself that he had anticipated a "hot" welcome.

The humid air blowing the casement drapes by the open patio door caught his attention. "Johanna?"

He found her lying prone on the sofa, resembling a broiled lobster, snoring softly. When he touched her sunbaked flesh she stirred drowsily.

"Do you prefer your eggs sunnyside up or over easy?" he queried, smiling at the look of sleepy delight on her face when she saw him.

"Scrambled," she hinted, wondering if he was going to fix breakfast. "Turn down the air conditioner when you leave," she slurred.

"Johanna! You've *fried* yourself," Charles said, his voice showing concern. When he released her arm, a white print remained against her fiery red skin.

"Charles?" Disoriented by the heat and the tight, prickly sensation on her shoulder, she sat up, facing the blinding sun. She groaned as she realized she had foolishly fallen sound asleep, unprotected by lotion, in the brilliant summer sun. The groan increased in volume when she glanced down and saw the results.

"Hurt?"

"Terribly," she confessed, unable to keep from wincing when she swung her feet down. "The tips of my toes are burned," she whispered dryly.

Charles bent down, scooped her into his arms and, careful to touch only the side that had lain against the sofa, carried her into the condo. "Do you have some Solarcaine?" he asked as he took her straight into her bedroom.

"I never burn—much," she moaned, testing the angry red skin lightly with her fingertips.

"You're lucky you don't have heatstroke. What would have happened if I had gone by my place first?"

Elevating one leg, she grimaced. She couldn't answer his question, not when her kneecaps threatened to blister and fall on the floor. The cool air blowing from the vent near the ceiling made a shiver course across her overheated skin.

"I'm freezing and burning up at the same time," she complained, crossing her arms over her chest.

"You stay put," Charles instructed, worried. "I'll check out the medicine cabinet." He picked up the satin comforter from the end of the bed and lightly drew it up to her chin.

Minutes later, a bottle of burn lotion in one hand, a glass of tepid water and aspirin in the other, he sat down on the edge of the bed.

"Take these and drink all the water," he encouraged. "Then I'll put this lotion on."

Johanna lifted her head off the pillow and acquiesced with demur, swallowing the pill, then emptying the glass in thirsty gulps.

"Easy. Too much water too fast and you'll be sick to your stomach."

With one hand holding a puddle of creamy pink lotion, he lowered the comforter with the other. *Where do I start?* he pondered. Her toes, knees, eyelids, and the skin bordering her scanty suit were a dark, vivid red.

"This should help," he soothed, starting with her feet.

"Nothing will help," she moaned fatalistically. "Terminal sunburn." The light coat of lotion, however, was beginning to relieve the burning sensation.

Charles chuckled in response to her diagnosis. "On a vacation trip to Florida I tried to compete with a pork rind for crispiness," he joked, wanting to distract her from the discomfort as his hand soaked her kneecaps. "Took the lead out of my pencil for a week. Bending my legs to walk was a test of fortitude."

"I'm red one day, tanned the next," she reassured him.

"Not this time, lady," he contradicted, soothing the lotion on her inflamed upper thighs. "Lift your hips. I'll have to take your suit off."

Modesty ingrained from childhood made her protest weakly. "I'll do it."

"Don't be silly. You can't open your eyes to see, much less apply the lotion. Much as I ad-

168

mire your delectable body, I make it a rule never to rape a charred woman."

Hips raised, she was too miserable to retort or make an issue of it. She felt him carefully ease the swimsuit off.

"Was that a lustful gasp I heard?" she asked in a mocking voice.

"No," he whispered. The livid contrast of white and red skin made the sunburn appear even worse. His own skin prickled in empathy. He wished he could absorb her pain as he poured lotion on the swimsuit line. Tenderly, the tips of his fingers traced the line. Consciously blanketing his mind from any sensuous thoughts, he spread it over her midriff, then, clasping the front hook of the bikini top, he sighed deeply. The pungent fragrance of wintergreen brought him back to his senses. Mentally he acknowledged his weakness as he gently covered the portion of her body to which he had ministered.

A smile wavered on Johanna's lips. "Good thing I'm too inhibited to sunbathe topless."

Hiding his shaking hands, Charles cursed his lack of control. *Pretty poor specimen of a man who can't discipline his own hands. How am I going to make it out the door knowing she is naked beneath this cover? Not a multiple-choice question,* he silently groaned as he felt his loins tighten, responding to merely the image of the fullness of her breasts and her long legs.

Johanna blindly snaked her hand around the nape of his neck. "Sorry about this. I had great plans for this afternoon."

He captured her forearm and kissed the unburned underside. "My intentions are honorable," he admitted, "but I'm struggling."

He smoothed the fluid on the arm he had held, then lowered it under the cover. Lightly stroking the burned portion of her face, he attempted to end the building tension in his body with a joke.

"Tryouts with Santa"—one finger whisked over her beacon red nose—"are at eight o'clock tonight."

"Rudolph will be job hunting on Christmas Eve," she quipped.

"Yeah, but Santa won't be making any deliveries if he has you along," he teased, looking for a place to wipe his oily hands.

He spied a box of tissues on the bedside table, plucked three from the container, and wiped his fingers and palms.

"How is it you can make me laugh when my body is suffering the slings and arrows of ultraviolet rays?" she questioned.

"Easily. Laughter is the saline solution for life and an optometrist. It refreshes . . . makes you feel alive." He bent over her and nestled a kiss in the softness of her hair. "We'll never be bored at the breakfast table."

"Mmmm," she hummed, the relief from the lotion making her complacent. "What are we doing for the rest of the day today?"

"I scheduled a nap with you wrapped around me, but it was burned off the agenda. Any suggestions?"

Lying naked within inches of Charles, she found her mind willing but the flesh unable. The erogenous, unburned portions of her body tingled as though betrayed by the defunct sun-blocking pigment of the burned area. What could she do?

"I'll fix you lunch," she offered.

Grinning devilishly, Charles tossed the soiled tissues in the waste can and altered the offer. "I'll fix lunch, and you can sit at the table in a *Hustler* pose," he teased, knowing she wouldn't be able to stand clothing against her skin.

"You're too *handy* in the kitchen," she tweaked, attempting a poor pun.

A long, lazy, non-touch afternoon stretched behind them. Charles ordered pizza from a nearby restaurant when he had the choice of going to the grocery store to shop or ordering out and staying with Johanna. The companionable evening was spent talking, laughing, playing gin rummy, and just past the ten o'clock news program, Johanna wondered how she had existed during the years they had been apart.

Charles yawned, arms stretched out to his sides, high above his head. "Bedtime. Some wicked woman has kept me up all night, then denied me a nap, and I'm"—he yawned again—"exhausted." His eyes skimmed over the Chinese silk robe loosely wrapped around Johanna's slender form. "The night will be agony if I stay," he said, abruptly rising to his feet. "I'd be scared to death of rolling over and hitting your sunburn."

"Stay. I'll sleep on the sofa. You can have the bed," Johanna offered, not willing to see him depart.

Charles took his jacket out of the front closet and shook his head negatively, saying, "Straws stuck under the fingernails would be preferable to knowing you're in the next room sleeping. I've suffered through two weeks. Two or three more days . . ." His sentence dwindled to nothingness.

Stiffleggedly crossing the width of the room, Johanna joined him by the front door. "I heal quickly," she promised.

Lightly circling his arms around her waist, their chests barely touching, he kissed the hair by her temple. "Who would believe, when I said

172

I would never hurt you I was speaking of physically rather than emotionally?" A loving pat placed on her unburned bottom, he said, "Can I take up residency during the peeling stage of your affliction?"

"You want to live with a flaky woman?" she teased, stretching up on tiptoe to brush her lips against his after-five shadow.

"Most definitely," he murmured, stepping back toward the door. "Lock up. Call me first thing in the morning with a medical bulletin."

Johanna leaned against the door, grumbling to herself after he had left. "Heck of a time to come up half-baked!"

Thursday, skin recovered, Johanna spent the day getting ready for "the big night" they had joked about since "baking day." She had spent hours planning the scene down to the last romantic detail.

Charles would arrive, she fantasized, open the door with the key she had given him, and walk into a room brimming with the scent of flowers. The lights would be turned down, but not far enough for him to stumble and impale himself on the umbrella rack. Soft music, classical, would be playing on the tape deck. The petals she had plucked from several roses made a scent-filled path from the door to the bedroom.

Smiling to herself as she imagined the look on his face, she visualized herself seductively lounging on the bed in her black, cobweb lace lounging gown, which would be highlighted by the pure white satin coverlet she had also bought. Crystal champagne glasses were strategically placed on a silver tray beside the silver wine holder and beneath the flickering candles in the candelabra.

Hair and body fragrant, Johanna stuck her head out the bathroom door and peeked at the clock. Half an hour, she clocked, brushing her dark hair until it appeared to glow with a moonbeam sheen. The lacy confection she wore clung in all the right places. The moisturizer she had drenched herself in had prevented her skin from peeling too badly. Teeny, dry blisters speckled her toes, knees, and upper arms but could only be detected upon close inspection. Her hands molded the lace over her rounded hips, and the grin she had concealed throughout the day burst forth, spreading her lips into the widest of toothy grins.

Heart aflutter, eager anticipation painted a natural pink tinge over her high cheekbones. The coolness of the coverlet soothed the heated flush of her body as she reclined provocatively, her leg stretched out and slightly bent.

"Johanna. I'm home," Charles called from the doorway. "Where are . . ."

The soft rose petals on the floor answered his question. The primitive urges below his belt made him hurry across the room, and his mental facilities took over in the short seconds it took to reach the doorway.

"Tonight the night?" he asked, voice husky with the desire his mind could not control. Mentally he calculated: Had it been a month since Johanna first appeared in his office unexpectedly? Quick mathematical figuring added up to twenty-eight with the speed of a calculator. She was ready to get pregnant! Was this sexy attitude part of her plan?

Imitating the seductive movements of a model doing mattress commercials, Johanna languidly raised one bent arm over her head. The smile on her face and the inviting curves of her body mutely beckoned him. Watching her, he saw the gleam of desire sparkling between her dark-fringed eyelashes.

She expected him to begin disrobing or comment on the alluring picture she had created. Something . . . anything other than nonchalantly leaning against the doorjamb as though the room would collapse if he moved toward her. Hadn't the previous days when she had been too burned to make love been a chaotic blend of anticipation and sexual tension? Didn't he know a romantic setting when he saw one?

Pouting her lips seductively, she said in an amused tone, "I couldn't get delivery on the ceiling mirrors." Sliding one hand over the filmy, black lace covering, she accentuated her feminine attributes.

Charles, with the stiffness of a programmed robot, crossed the room silently. Bracing himself over her supple form, which immediately curved toward him, he asked softly, "Are we making love? Or making babies?"

"Both?" Johanna teased, wanting the tense lines around his mouth to dissipate. "Aren't you warm with all those clothes on?" she hinted, fiddling playfully with the buckle on his belt.

"Mmmm," Charles answered wryly as he straightened and removed his suit jacket. "Sexy nightie? Soft music?" Spotting the wine, he lifted it out of the silver bucket. "Good year," he commented abstractedly, not knowing whether it was or not. "Why the trappings if you'd settle for a clinical, no-nonsense impregnation?" His hand swept in a wide arc to encompass the room. "Why?"

"Plan *A*'s setting wasn't restricted to . . . a camp cot," she defended, patting the side of the bed and becoming more and more impatient to be held in his arms. This was a hell of a time to

176

discuss plans she had discarded earlier in the week. Was he intentionally picking a fight? Had he changed his mind about wanting to live with her?

Watching Charles begin to jerkily disrobe, she felt relief flood over her. She must have misinterpreted his coolness. *Maybe I overdid the flowers after all,* she mused, resting her head back against the pillow. In one sharp tug Charles pulled his shirttail from beneath his belt.

Lazily, Johanna fanned her dark hair over the pillowcase as she remembered him noticing the effect on their first night together. She thirstily drank in each inch of skin exposed by his fingers, hastily unbuttoning his shirt.

The white ring circling his tautly clamped lips made her smile wider. *He's struggling for control. If he could have seen the erotic images I've imagined all day, he wouldn't be worried about rushing me,* she thought, nearly chuckling.

"Adding the romantic elements makes it . . ." *Hypocritical,* Charles thought, thoroughly disgusted. Johanna couldn't wait to patiently work out their different attitudes about parenthood. In typical schoolmarm fashion, he condemned, she had provided a warm classroom to meet her objectives. *Damn her goals,* he silently cursed. *I'm here, frothing at the*

*mouth for love and affection and she wants . . .
a baby*.

"Exciting?" Johanna said in a lilting voice, completing his sentence.

He hurled his shirt into the corner of the room as he made his decision. Johanna had no inhibitions about using him. By damn, the teacher needed a lesson in alternative plans.

Masking his inward rage with a smile, he sauntered to the bed. His hands trembled from suppressed anger as he raked his knuckles over the sheer lace slanting from shoulder to waist. The cat-who-ate-the-canary grin on her face made his blood boil. *If I didn't love her, I'd probably strangle her*. The soft fullness of the breast beneath his hand made his manhood leap to a life of its own, straining against the zipper of his slacks.

"Nice hands," Johanna appreciatively whispered, tracing the tanned flesh above his belt with one fingertip. *The muscle ticking over his jaw is a dead giveaway,* she mused. Knowing he was restraining the pace of their lovemaking at his own cost was the highest compliment a man could pay his woman.

The bed sank beneath his weight as he sat, then leaned over her. Johanna closed her eyes as his dark head bent to nuzzle the shadow between her breasts. Short, pecklike kisses claimed her neck. The sharp tug on her scalp as he wound his fingers into her hair made her own fingernails dig into the back muscles she had been stroking.

"Johanna . . ." His voice shook despite his effort to keep it under control. He had to test her love for him the only way he knew how. "I should have told you . . . five years ago I had a vasectomy."

"What?" she murmured, not hearing anything over the blood rushing into her ears, not wanting to talk, only wanting to satisfy the craving ache below the pit of her belly. Taking his hand, she pressed his palm against the heat of her body and arched beneath his curving fingers. Rubbing her hand over the knuckles, she concentrated on willing him to touch her, to make the desert winds blow once again.

Charles's anger erupted. He knew she was caught up in the pursuit of her goals and hadn't even heard his fraudulent confession. Shoving away, he hastily grabbed his shirt and jacket. He refused to respond to Johanna calling his name as he hurriedly rushed out of her home.

Swearing under his breath, he said aloud, "Any court would see it as justifiable homicide!"

Pitching his clothes in the backseat, he climbed in the car, twisted the key, and peeled out of the parking lot. "Out of her life," he growled, disgusted, angry . . . and hurt.

The miles between them were driven swiftly. Clamoring out of his car, Charles ran to the sanctity of his own home. Once inside he slammed the door shut. Johanna had cut his heart out with the swiftness of a laser beam. The phone ringing broke through his self-recriminating curses. Yanking the cord from the wall, he flung it against the wall. The crashing noise sounded good to his ears.

He strode to the fireplace mantel, and with one arm, knocked the pewter candlesticks to the floor, raking his knuckles against the harsh surface of the bricks. The Eli Terry mantel clock chimed twice before it smashed against the wall.

The rage Charles felt was uncaged. His iron bars of control had snapped. Blindly, uncaring, he heaved every unattached object his fingers touched against the walls and the furniture.

Stomach twisting, cramping, he stumbled into the bedroom and flung himself on the bed. A roar of anguished pain pierced the room as he pounded the pillow with his fist. Shoulders shaking convulsively, he despised the hot scratchiness behind his tightly shut eyelids.

"Damned fool," he cursed, the poison of her betrayal rampantly coursing through his shuddering frame with the impact of acid. "Thought she loved you!" The pillow rocketed, jet-propelled, through the air, destroying everything in its path. The rampage ended as abruptly as it had begun.

Rolling onto his back, Charles stared stonily at the ceiling. Johanna, lying on the bed, superimposed herself on the creamy whiteness. Forearm crossing his eyes, he destroyed the image as he had the contents of his home.

Why doesn't she want more of me than stud service? he questioned in despair. *Had her response been faked all along? Hadn't they shared more than sex?* Charles shook his head, not willing to accept those possibilities. *It isn't fair,* his mind screamed at the injustice.

"We would have had a chance for it all!" he moaned. "Love, marriage, *and* children."

I made the same damned mistake fifteen years ago. Too much, too little, too late, he thought, bludgeoning himself. *Too much passion, too little love, and too late with a proposal . . . again!*

"Should have gone down on bended knee when we were at the farm," he said to himself between tight lips. "No," he argued abruptly. Swinging his legs to the side of the bed, elbows propped on his knees, he plowed furrows through his hair with his fingers.

Sex, baby, marriage, heartache, all spun

181

around in his brain with nightmarish quality. The heels of his hands ground into his eye sockets to stop the spinning, but he couldn't get relief . . . he felt the pain all the way to his chest.

"Numbskull . . . should have run like hell when she first walked into the office!" He knew he was taking a chance, but, oh, Lord, it hurt so much to lose again. And he knew he had lost.

A shroud of black depression cloaked his bent shoulders as he fell back on the bed, hands shielding his face. "I loved her . . . love her . . . lost her."

He didn't notice the salty tears washing his face. The spread fingers and palms would not absorb their moisture. Misery blocked any sense of sight, touch, or sound.

He didn't hear the front door open. He didn't smell the perfume on Johanna. He didn't see her enter the room and stand silently by the bed.

During the short time spent behind the wheel of her car, Johanna had tried to sort through the disaster her romantic seduction had turned into. Pride had not placed any roadblocks between her condo and Charles's house.

Baffled and confused by his abrupt departure, it had taken several seconds to fully realize what he had said. He had left because, being sterile, he could not make her dreams a reality. Didn't he know she no longer cared about anything other than the two of them being together? Johanna surmised instantly that he didn't.

Staring at the tears sliding down the side of his hand, slowly disappearing into the dark hairs on his wrist and arm, she loved him more than life itself.

"I love you, Charles," she whispered. "You're all I want . . . all I need."

Charles rolled to his stomach, palms over his ears to block out the words his mind had conjured up from nowhere. *Am I going completely out of my mind?* Sniffing, he could smell Estee Lauder. *Insane,* he thought, inhaling the fragrance as though it were life-giving air to a drowning man.

"Do you want me to leave?" Johanna asked timidly when she saw him turn away. Her dark eyes clouded with tears; she wasn't certain she could leave.

"No," Charles muttered, wondering if the hallucination would stay with him throughout his madness. Sighing heavily, he wished it were possible. Blindly his arms opened, reaching for the elusive dream.

Johanna shed the trench coat she had hastily thrown on, and knelt on the bed, then slipped into his arms.

"Crazy," he muttered into the silkiness of her

hair. "No wonder the mental asylums are over-crowded."

Charles truly believed he hovered on the brink between reality and insanity. Crushing his dream woman to his chest, he opened his eyes. Blinking, again and again, he couldn't believe his eyes.

"What are you doing here?" he managed to croak, dragging her up until their eyes were level.

"Chasing a dream, maybe," she replied hesitantly. "Charles Franklin, I love you. Above all else, I want you to know that." Her fingers wiped away the last traces of moisture as she asked, "Will you make an honest woman of me?"

"Yes," he answered simply.

Needing to clear the air of any misunderstandings, she said, "No more Plan *A, B, or C.*"

"O period, K period," he agreed, kissing her tenderly. His last thought was O for Our; K for kids.

EPILOGUE

"Ten years of loving, three children crawlin',
two horses pawin', one golden ring," Charles
improvised to the tune of "The Twelve Days of
Christmas" as he climbed the stepladder to
place the final ornament on their tall, bushy tree
in the center of the bay window.

Johanna's smile beamed brighter than the
miniature lights flashing on the tree. "Bragging,
Mr. Franklin?"

"Can't . . . didn't father all of them," he
teased, jumping nimbly to the floor.

"Ah, the old vasectomy story again?" she
asked, winding her arms around his neck and
swishing the length of her red taffeta skirt

against his thighs. "Three boys with *those*"—she fondly poked the tip of her finger in his dimples —"a carbon copy that can't be denied."

Charles tossed his head back, laughing, his hands cupping the roundness of her bottom possessively. "The boys I'll claim, but those mares . . . unh-unh!"

Contentedly sighing, Johanna held him close, listening to his strong, solid heartbeat. "Happy?"

"Is Santa full of ho-ho-hos?" he replied, brushing his lips over her short, feathered bangs. "Love, unless you plan on taking out your contacts and calling off the party, you'd better quit swaying against me."

It was Johanna's turn to laugh. "Speaking of contacts, when do I get those new kind I can wear to bed?" Her pelvic bones rocked back and forth, teasing the growing hardness pressing her rounded stomach.

"Old married women with a passel of kids should wear wire-framed glasses like Mrs. Claus."

"Once you said you'd know I loved you when I threw away my glasses and wore contacts. And now?" With a shrug she started to unwind her arms.

"Now? Now, when my hairline is in danger of

meeting the point on my head, I have more important concerns."

"Such as?"

"Oh"—he paused thoughtfully—"keeping your fingers off my . . . plants."

"Plants or pants?" she whispered, dropping her arms and wedging her hands underneath his waistband.

"Writing poems . . ."

Wiggling her fingers lower, she giggled mischievously. A second later she was scooped over his shoulder, the flat of his hand rubbing and swatting her bottom as she squealed in protest.

"We have company coming! Put me down! We don't have time!"

Unceremoniously, Charles dumped her on their king-size bed and fell on top of her. He breathed heavily, "For us? There is always time."

And there was. Time was on their side . . . it always had been.

Look for Next Month's
Candlelight Ecstasy Romances®:

Candlelight Ecstasy Romances™

\$1.95 each

At your local bookstore or use this handy coupon for ordering:

 DELL BOOKS
P.O. BOX 1000. PINE BROOK. N.J. 07058-1000   B219A

Please send me the books I have checked above. I am enclosing \$_____ (please add 75c per copy to cover postage and handling). Send check or money order—no cash or C.O.D.'s. Please allow up to 8 weeks for shipment.

Name _____

Address _____

City _____ State/Zip _____

Candlelight
Ecstasy Romances™

$1.95 each